THE LOVER BOY

C-TREY JONES

THE LOVER BOY

Clarence Jones

ISBN 9798218125875 (trade paperback) | ISBN 9798218112202 (ebook)

Cover design by: Branden Rice
Library of Congress Control Number: 2018675309
Printed in the United States of America

First Printing, 2022

CONTENTS

CONTENTS

CONTENTS

Acknowledgments

About The Author
222

THE GOLDEN GIRL

My name is Roman Richardson, and I'm a romance addict. Well, as much of a romance addict as you can be when you're a 20 year old virgin who's never been in a serious relationship. I often feel like I'm haunted by my potential. I feel as if I'm destined to be someone great, and I have an obligation to live up to that. At least, that's what I tell myself. The reality of my current life is different though. It's like I'm standing at the bottom of Mt. Everest, looking up at the future version of myself who somehow made it to the top. The current version of me always seems to mess up when it matters most, especially when it comes to women. The mountain that leads to my future self seems to get bigger and bigger with every failure or setback.

My love life has gone so far past tragic that it's starting to enter comedy territory. Not like the romantic comedies I grew up watching and wishing I could be a part of, but more like a parody version of that, a version where the protagonist's mere presence seemingly repels any woman within a 10 mile radius.

This is what races through my mind as the May sun beams down on me. I'm sitting outside, reading a Batman comic, waiting to get picked up to go home for the summer. The bench I'm sitting on is in the middle of the quad, surrounded by tall dorms. The campus is full of life, there is a sea of students getting their stuff together to leave. It was a long, stressful semester so I'm happy to be going home. I'm watching the cars and people pass, enjoying my last few moments on campus when all of a sudden, time slows down. It's the middle of May so it's already hot, but at that moment, the temperature increases even more and the light shifts towards one person.

She is the most beautiful girl I've ever seen. She has dark curly hair, luminous honey brown eyes that look almost golden in the sunlight, and olive, brown skin. At that moment she glances over at me and gives me a slight smile, but her eyes are red and puffy. You can tell she had just been crying. In spite of that, I feel my insides melt. It feels like she is the sun, and I'm seeing it for the first time. Despite the tears, she moves with such confidence and purpose. She has this aura that's ethereal and angelic. I can't take my eyes off of her. I'm not sure what's going on, but it feels like some kind of divine intervention. I have to talk to her.

My whole life I've spent in the background, passively watching others around me do things that I wish I could do, mainly, go after women. I went into college expecting to meet lots of new people, but so far all I've done is watch from the sideline. My roommate, Tristan, has no trouble in that regard. Every weekend he comes back to our dorm with a new girl, meanwhile I'm surrounded by women every day, at the gym, in class, at the dining hall, but I'm too afraid to even say hello. I can't help but feel weak and pathetic. Why do I have to be so passive and shy? But this feels like a shift. An opportunity to right past wrongs, to take 10 steps forward into being the person I'm meant to be. This girl, this moment, feels like a gift from the universe. She is the sun, and this is my moment to step into the sunlight.

By this point she's already past me and I have a decision to make. So many versions of me in the past would've just let her go, live to fight another day, not wanting to risk rejection, and then look back on the moment with self loathing and a hopeless desire to reverse time. Maybe I'm just meant to observe and watch from the sideline. After all, it's comfortable there, I can't get rejected if I never make a move. In spite of the subtle push I feel I'm getting, I also feel doubtful, like maybe this is just the universe's way of burying me even further into the ground. I can't help but think about how crushing this rejection would feel if things don't turn out the way I want. But then again the feeling of letting this opportunity slip away would feel much worse. And the opportunity is almost gone. She's like a balloon slowly floating up into the sky, soon to be out of my reach.

The only thing I know for sure is that I want her. I want to prove to myself that I can make this happen. So I muster up every ounce of strength and courage that I can muster and I go after her.

As I'm approaching the mystery girl, I'm hyper aware of all the students around me. I can't help but think about how embarrassing it would be if she rejected me in front of all these people, but it's too late to turn back now. Right before I get to her, I see my dad's car in the corner of my eye. I hesitate. It feels like I just crashed back down to reality. All of my courage and confidence evaporates. In that same moment she turns around and sees me. Her radiant, golden, honey brown eyes lock onto mine, and I lose myself. I forget how to think, I forget how to speak. For a second I just stare at her dumbfounded not knowing what to do.

"Have a good summer." I manage to say in a barely audible whisper. Before she can respond I turn to walk back to get my things. Hanging my head in shame.

I walk over to my dad's car and load up my things.

"Hey Rome, how was your semester?" Asks my dad, as he starts to pull out of the loading area. Growing up I was often told how much I looked like my dad. We have the same deep, russet brown eyes, the same rugged jawline, the same easy smile, but to differing effects. My dad is a burly, gregarious man, and when he smiles, he lights up a room, the energy is infectious. In high school, a lot of the girls in my class would jokingly ask me to set them up with him. My smile is more meek, and understated, which is probably why I didn't have a similar effect on those same girls.

"It was fine." I reply, still noticeably distracted by the scene that just played out with the mystery girl.

"What's wrong, Rome? You seem a little off."

"I think I just blew it with this girl." I reply, trying not to sound too dejected.

"There's very little in this world that requires more courage than approaching a woman you like," my dad says. "But, when the time is right it'll just feel natural and flow easily."

His words make me feel a little better, but I can tell this failure is going to stick with me for a while. I try to tell myself that it wasn't the right time to shoot my shot. She was crying after all. She probably wasn't interested anyway. But what if she was? What if I just blew the opportunity of a lifetime? What a failure I am. I replay the moment in my head over and over. "Have a good summer." What was that? Instead of a triumphant moment in the sun, I feel like I got caught in the rain without an umbrella. What a nice way to start my summer break.

THE COWORKER

It's the second week of summer and things aren't too bad. "No Scrubs" by TLC plays in the background as I'm getting ready for work. About halfway through the first chorus of the song, my phone rings. It's my roommate, Tristan. Tristan and I go way back, we'd been best friends since 3rd grade when we were both picked to be on the same basketball team at recess one day. All throughout grade school, Tristan had been Mr. Popular. He was the star of the basketball team, and as a tall light skin guy, he had his pick of girls to date. Tristan often has people tell him that he looks like a version of Kelly Oubre, the NBA player, with the same hairstyle and everything. On the other hand, I have medium brown skin, slightly darker than Tristan's, with a low cut fade. I'm also tall, well over six feet, but a couple of inches shorter than Tristan. So I spent most of my teen years being both literally and figuratively overlooked by people who wanted to be around Tristan instead. I always felt like his sidekick, but I'm grateful to be friends with him. The phone rings again, and I pick up.

"Hey, Rome how ya doing?" Tristan asks.

"I'm alright, just getting ready for work," I reply as I frantically look for another clean sock to wear.

"You're not still thinking about that girl from the quad, are you?"

There's an extended awkward pause as I try to think of how to respond.

"You've got to be kidding," says Tristan, clearly exasperated. "It's been 2 weeks, and you don't even know her. There's plenty of other fish in the sea."

"It doesn't matter how many fish there are if I don't feel confident enough to make a move."

"You just have to talk to them. You always overcomplicate things."

You just have to talk to them, I repeat in my head once I get off the phone with Tristan. That's easy for him to say. I often envied Tristan's effortless charm and charisma. I've always been way more reserved, with countless self esteem and confidence issues. It's one of the reasons I resonated so much with Batman growing up. He wasn't born or gifted with his abilities, he had to work for them. I may not have as much charm and charisma as guys like Tristan, but I'm determined to work and build myself up to be just as respectable. I want to dedicate this summer to working, making money, and getting a car. My goal was to keep my body as occupied as possible with work and exercise so that my brain didn't have time to think about my past failures with women, or any women for that matter. Little did I know that that was a futile wish. The universe had other plans.

I pull up to work, for my first official shift. I'm working at a thrift store, kind of like Goodwill, but under a different name. Tina, the owner, who also serves as the store manager, directs me to the back area which is where we accept donations.

The back room is basically a glorified warehouse. There is a huge stack of garbage bags off to the side which are donations we're meant to sort through, and tables set up around the room for us to sort through those donations to see what was usable to be sold in the store, and what was trash. There are about 3 tables total, and 2 employees per table. Most of my coworkers are older women in their 40s and 50s, except for one girl who looks to be about my age. She has rich brown eyes, dark skin, and braids pulled into a stylish ponytail. She has an athletic build, and the angel numbers 777 on her left wrist. The lighting in the warehouse area is terrible but she still looked very put together and glamorous. She's the only one that didn't have a partner with her at her table, but she'd already sorted through twice as many donations as any of the other employees.

"Alright Roman, I'm pairing you with Camryn," says Tina. "She's only been here a few months, but she's already the best worker here. She's scared off a couple of former employees here in the past, but as long as you do what she tells you to do, you should be okay."

I go over to my table and introduce myself to Camryn. She seems very standoffish. She cautiously looks at me, seemingly gauging what kind of worker I'll be. She explains what I'll be doing. For my job, I'll be accepting donations, sorting through the donations, and most importantly, making trash runs for all the donations that we couldn't accept.

I nervously grab a bag to start sorting. I have a history of messing up when I first start a new job, and I am determined not to have any mishaps this time. The work is boring, simple, and tedious, but it's kind of satisfying. I can feel Camryn's piercing eyes gazing at me while I sort through my first bag of donations. It's hard not to feel intimidated. Her intense stare makes me feel like I'm locked in a cage with a tiger and she is deciding whether I'm a friend or food. I feel like one minor slip up and I'll be done for. Despite all that, I feel a strong desire to impress her.

The other workers around us are having lively conversations, but Camryn and I continue to work in silence. Each of us waiting on the other to make the first move.

"You know we don't have to work in silence, right?" Camryn says, finally breaking the spell we were under for the past hour. She stares at me with those unsettling eyes, waiting for me to respond.

I feel anxious, like my response could make or break whatever this work relationship would be like.

"You mean to tell me we haven't been playing the quiet game for the past hour? That sucks, I thought I was about to win a prize or something," I responded dryly.

She glares at me with those unsettling brown eyes, with an expression that's hard for me to read, it's somewhere between disgust and mild amusement. "If that's your best attempt at sarcasm, maybe working in silence is better actually."

After a while, I see the trash cart is getting full so I decide to go take it out. Taking out the trash is a grueling process. I would have to roll the cart out to the back of this 18 wheeler, and throw the bags in one by one. The cart fits around a dozen or so trash bags and they all weigh a ton, not to mention the fact that it's summertime, so it's always going to be extremely hot outside. The whole process takes about 20 minutes, which I figure will also be enough time for things to get less tense between Camryn and I.

I load up the cart, making sure everything is secure, and then I'm off. I roll the cart out the door, and get to the ramp that you're supposed to pull the cart down to get it off the sidewalk so I can safely transport it to the truck, when disaster strikes. The cart isn't evenly distributed on the ramp so as I'm trying to pull it down, the whole cart starts to tip over. Soon, the cart fell with a loud thud, and half of the contents in the trash bags that I just secured, came spilling out onto the ground. All of the conversations the other workers are having stop, and they all stare at me, dumbfounded. I try my best to hide my shame, and pick every-thing up as quickly as possible.

As I make my way back from the truck, I can't help but feel embarrassed. All day I was worried about making a mistake and, of course, like clockwork, it came to fruition. So much for wanting to impress Camryn, she probably thinks I'm a joke now. I get back inside, and despite the air conditioning being on full blast, I'm sweating bullets.

"Wow Roman, who knew you were so graceful and coordinated," says Camryn sarcastically. "It's okay, that ramp has gotten the best of all of us at some point."

It looks like she is holding back a smile. For the first time all shift, I feel like she may have accepted me after all.

"Come on, man, you have to go, it's the first pool party of the summer," says Tristan as I pretend to be preoccupied with my phone.

It's a couple of days after my first day at work, and Tristan is trying to convince me to go to a pool party. I've been telling him no over text all day, so naturally, Tristan being Tristan, showed up to my house to convince me face to face. Tristan knows better than anyone, that if left to my own devices, I would just stay home all the time. As an introvert who doesn't drink or smoke, all the loud noises and drunk people can be off putting.

"Think of all the beautiful girls in bikinis that will be there. I need my wingman with me," says Tristan.

"You know that's not true," I reply, taking a break from my phone long enough to respond to his blasphemy. "Not once have you needed my help getting girls."

"Yeah yeah, but it's not as fun if you're not there with me."

"I'll think about it," I say as I go to look at my phone again.

"You'll think about it? The party is in 30 minutes," says Tristan as he snatches the phone from my hands.

"Come on, you know I need that. Cindy might have messaged me back, " I say as I reach for my phone.

"Forget about Cindy. Let me say it again. There's gonna be dozens of beautiful women in bikinis. Your phone can't give you that," proclaims Tristan. "Okay, maybe it can, but it's not as good as seeing it in person."

Cindy's a girl I met on Tinder, and truthfully, she hasn't responded to me in three days. I'm doubtful that she's planning on getting back to me, yet another dead end. Maybe there's someone at this pool party who's worth meeting.

"Okay, I'll go with you," I say with a defeated sigh. "But you owe me."

We open the gate to get into the pool, and immediately the familiar smell of chlorine and sunscreen hits like a ton of bricks. The song "Nice For What" by Drake blares over the speaker system as I take in the scene. The pool water is a brilliant shade of blue as the hot, June sun shines down on it. There are already a ton of people in the water. Tristan was right, there are a lot of beautiful women laying poolside on the tanning chairs, and in the water. Will I actually talk to any of them? Probably not, but it's nice knowing they're there.

Unlike me, Tristan isn't shy around women, so he immediately goes to talk to one of the girls sitting near us on one of the tanning chairs. So much for being his wingman, I think to myself as I look for a place to sit.

After 20 minutes or so, Tristan comes to where I'm sitting with a small piece of paper in his hand.

"Hey Rome, I got that blonde girl's number over there," he says while gesturing to a pretty blonde girl who's sitting with her feet in the water by the side of the pool. "Thanks for your help, you're the best wingman a guy could ask for," he says with a grin.

"I literally didn't do anything," I say as I continue scrolling through Twitter.

"You came, man, you know you're my good luck charm," says Tristan earnestly.

"Yeah yeah, well I need some of my good luck to rub off on me for once," I say jokingly.

"How are you though? Are you having a good time?" asks Tristan.

I take a moment to consider his question. It's uncomfortably hot out, and all the seats with umbrellas were taken by the time we got here, so I feel myself starting to sweat. On the other hand, there's good music playing, and plenty of pretty women around, so overall I'd say it was a good time.

"You know what, I'm having a nice time," I say with a shrug.

We spend the next few minutes people watching. Tristan has a couple beers that seem to appear magically from thin air. While I stick to my *Simply Lemonade* bottle. I'm sitting, contently with Tristan when I hear a girl's voice.

"Hey," I hear someone call out from the side of me. Surely they're calling for Tristan, no girl ever calls for me. "Hey, Roman," the girl repeats sharply.

I turn, and my confusion turns into pleasant surprise as I see my new coworker, Camryn coming my way. The same Camryn that I made a fool of myself in front of, a couple days ago. She's wearing a bikini top and small jean shorts.

"Oh, hey Camryn. I didn't expect to see you here."

"Oh, you think I just spend all of my time sorting through donation bags at work?" Camryn asks sarcastically. "I could say the same for you though. You don't seem like the pool party type."

"Yeah, my friend dragged me out here," I say, remembering that I had forgotten to introduce them. "Camryn, this is Tristan. Tristan, this is Camryn."

"Nice to meet you," says Tristan, giving a small nod.

"Same to you," says Camryn. "Well, I'll let you get back to it. I hope that lemonade doesn't have you too hungover at work tomorrow," Camryn says, gesturing to the bottle I'm holding. "Oh, and don't go crashing any trash carts out here, we're all trying to have a nice time," she says with a grin before walking off to her group of friends at the other end of the pool.

"Hmm, she's cute," says Tristan, before going off to get another beer.

CHAPTER

3

DATING APPS

I'd been working at the thrift store for a few weeks and every shift, Camryn has started bringing up some random topic. Ever since our impromptu meeting at the pool party, it feels as if she's made it her personal mission to get me to open up to her anyway she can. She's already gotten me to admit that I'm trying to create my own graphic novel, which is something I've only told Tristan about. It's been a dream of mine to start my own graphic novel, and I've been working on a shorter, comic version to submit into different competitions as a way to practice.

Most of the time I'm not sure how to respond to Camryn when she brings up these random topics, but it's helped me learn more about her. She's a sophomore in college and she studies exercise science. She had a soccer scholarship but she had a serious knee injury her freshman year and had to leave the team. She also has a boyfriend that she's been with for over three years.

That boyfriend part made me feel like a weight had been lifted off my chest. I'm not one of those people that thinks men and women can't be friends, but it definitely makes it easier when one of them is in an established relationship. Whenever I'm around single women, I feel almost obligated to create imaginary scenarios where we end up together. But now all the pressure's off, I don't have to try to impress her outside of the work lens.

Camryn likes to comment about how quiet and hard to read I am, which is something I've heard a lot over the years. Secretly I feel like my reserved demeanor is put on to help disguise my natural awkwardness. Initially I thought Camryn would be uptight and demanding, and when it comes to work she can definitely be a perfectionist, always liking things to be done a certain way. Her natural tone is also somewhat confrontational, and most of our other coworkers don't seem to like her much. Despite that, it seems like I've passed whatever imaginary test she had in her mind, and she's taken an interest in me. I can feel myself warming up to her.

"What do you have planned for the weekend?" I ask. Camryn and I have the weekend off, and we're both trying to find ways to make the last 30 minutes of our shift go by faster.

"My boyfriend and I are going to this nice resort by the beach. We're gonna go to the casino, get massages, and have a romantic dinner by the water. It's gonna be great" Camryn says excitedly. "It's my first time seeing him since the summer started. What about you? What do you have planned?"

"Normally, I wouldn't have anything planned, but this weekend Tristan and I are going on a double date at the bowling alley," I reply.

Double dates with Tristan are a mixed bag. On one hand, I'm exposed to a caliber of woman I wouldn't be exposed to otherwise. But on the other hand, my reserved and socially awkward nature often gets overshadowed by Tristan's natural charisma. Overall I'm feeling optimistic, but I know ultimately it's unlikely anything substantial will come from it.

"That sounds fun," Camryn replies enthusiastically. "I didn't know you'd been seeing someone recently."

"I haven't. It's a blind date."

"Oh," says Camryn hesitantly. "Blind dates can be risky."

"Yeah, but I trust Tristan's taste. He usually makes sure there's a cute girl for me." Usually, the issue isn't that the girl is too unattractive for me, it's that she's unwilling to go out with me again after the double date is over. I'm too ashamed to admit this to Camryn right now though.

"Well good luck, I hope things work out for you," replies Camryn.

Once our shifts are over she excitedly goes to her car to leave. After about 15 minutes, my Uber finally arrives to take me home, and after a couple of minutes of aimlessly scrolling through Instagram and Twitter, I get on Tinder. Nothing makes me feel more empty inside than being on dating apps. Part of me feels like I'm swiping my life away, the other part feels like the right girl could be one swipe away. When I first got on dating apps, I was wildly optimistic. A friend with benefits, a girlfriend, a wife, the possibilities were endless. It didn't take long for my optimism to fade. Dating apps are basically video games filled with women who don't actually exist. There are hundreds of options, but the chances of actually meeting someone worthwhile are low. Plus, all the options force you into a vicious cycle where you feel like you can always do better even though you can't really. Even if you miraculously match with someone who you feel has potential, the odds that you ever actually meet in person are slim.

In a way, dating apps are poisonous, and extremely backwards. When has bringing in more options ever helped someone narrow down their decision? At that moment I'm envious of Tristan. People like Tristan don't have to resort to things like double dates or dating apps to meet people, and if they do, it's almost like a separate reality for them. It's different for me. In an ideal world,

I'd just be able to meet someone naturally, in person, like in the olden days, but for an introverted guy like myself, who's afraid to make the first move, I just have to hope for the best. It's like a potentially fatal poison with a slim chance of curing an otherwise terminal illness. Or like putting yourself in debt with credit cards, or student loans, in order to put yourself in position to make more money. How bleak. I can't help but hate myself a little for feeling any kind of excitement when I get new matches.

A week earlier, I matched with a girl named Jade, and things were moving along pretty well. The rare time you match with someone and you actually see the potential. We made plans to go out to dinner, and of course, a couple days before we were supposed to meet, she stopped replying. Typical. Suddenly I'm not feeling as good about the double date with Tristan. Why should I expect anything different tonight? Maybe I'm just cursed. As I'm reflecting on what happened with Jade, my Uber pulls up to my house. I thank the driver and head inside. As I'm getting inside, I get a call from Tristan.

"Yo, you ready for tonight?" Tristan asks. "I'm picking you up in an hour."

"Yeah, I'll be ready," I say as I try to hide how dejected I've suddenly become. Unfortunately for me, unlike Camryn, Tristan knows me well enough to know when I'm feeling down.

"What's wrong, did you spill all the trash at work again?" Tristan asks.

There's a slight pause. I actually did knock over the trash cart again earlier in the week, but I couldn't let Tristan know that.

"No, I'm just feeling a little cynical."

"Well you gotta snap out of it. For both of our sakes. Let's have a good time tonight."

I decide Tristan's right. There's no reason I should allow Jade, or any other Tinder girls, to ruin my good time. Who knows, maybe the universe made Jade ghost me so that I could have a good time with an even cooler girl tonight. I hang up the phone and go get ready.

Tristan comes to get me, and he's blasting a song by Future. I get in the car and we roll out, my optimism for the night slowly returning. We pull up to the bowling alley, and the parking lot seems to be pretty full. "They're here already," says Tristan. We get out of the car to go inside. Once we get in we're greeted by 2 girls. One is a tall blonde girl who looks like she could be an instagram model. I remember her from the pool party a few weeks ago, she's the girl who's number Tristan was so excited about getting that day. The girl next to her is on the shorter side with faux locs, and just as pretty, but in a girl next door kind of way. She looks kind of familiar, but I can't figure out where I know her from.

"Roman this is Mackenzie," says Tristan, gesturing towards the tall blonde girl. "And this is–"

"Jade," I say, suddenly realizing where I knew her from. Jade, the girl from Tinder.

THE DOUBLE DATE

The bowling alley is dimly lit, most of the light shines on the individual lanes and pins. Good thing for me because I can feel what seems to be a tsunami of sweat pouring down my face as I burn with embarrassment. Of all the girls, why did it have to be this one? The sound of pins being knocked over echoes in the background. Part of me feels like one of those pins. Standing helpless, hoping to somehow remain standing after being obliterated by the unstoppable bowling ball that is the universe.

We are split into two separate teams, Tristan and Mackenzie against Jade and I. Sitting on the bench across from us, Tristan has his arm around Mackenzie and says something to her. She flashes him a smile and laughs softly. On the flipside, me and Jade are sitting as far apart as possible on our bench, barely within ear shot. A few minutes earlier, after Tristan had "introduced" us, I could see based on Jade's facial expression, that she recognized me right away and she did not look at all happy about it. Once we got to our lane we made some small talk, but it was excruciatingly awkward. Now Jade is sitting as far away from me as she could, on her phone, probably wishing she was anywhere else but here.

A small part of me thinks that maybe this is a second chance for me. After all, she liked me enough initially to match with me on Tinder, so maybe this is my chance to fix whatever I screwed up. The other, bigger part of me feels like this is just an unfortunate coincidence that can only end badly for me.

Tristan is the first person up, and he bowls a spare. Mackenzie is next and she knocks down eight of the pins. Jade goes and knocks down five of the pins, and now it's my turn. It's been a while since I last bowled, but I feel like this is my time to shine. Maybe Jade has a secret bowler fetish that I don't know about. Either way I definitely don't want to make a fool of myself in front of this girl. I guess I really don't have anything to lose, Jade probably won't like me any more regardless of the outcome, but I still feel the nerves coursing through my body and the pressure starts to build. I grab my ball and slowly make my way to the top of the lane. As I let go of the ball it feels perfect, it looks like it's going right down the middle. All of a sudden the ball starts to curve, by the time it gets to the end it misses all of the pins and spins right into the gutter. I go into the next roll in my turn, determined to knock down at least one pin, but the result was the same. I head back to the bench, completely dejected.

I had a couple more turns, all of them gutter balls. Now we're down big. I can feel the disappointment radiating off of Jade, and piercing me like shrapnel. I go up to bowl again, at this point I'm just ready to get this over with and go home. I hear Tristan yell out "Come on Roman, you got this! You're supposed to be trying to knock over the pins, stop aiming for the gutter." He's smiling, laughing, having a good time with Mackenzie. How can things be so easy for him and so hard for me? My vision becomes tinged with crimson as I feel what seems to be anger and jealousy racing through my body.

I love Tristan, and I've known him for most of my life, but it's tiring always being an afterthought around him. Growing up, whenever we'd play video games, card games, one on one in basketball, or any sort of competition, Tristan almost always won. He was the star, and people have always treated me like I was inferior to him. Even though he never treated me like I was inferior, everyone else's treatment weighed on me over the years to the point where I started to think that maybe I was. I look over at him with the beautiful girl next to him who's completely smitten by him, contrasted with the night I'm having and I'm overcome with a desire to beat him. Even though things with Jade are almost certainly not going to go my way, I'm determined to not end the night feeling like an afterthought or a loser. I go to roll the ball.

The satisfying sound of pins falling echoes throughout the bowling alley, but this time, the source of the sound is coming from my lane. I roll a strike. A few minutes later, I go up and roll another strike. Then another. Now I'm in the zone, I feel unstoppable, like I can do anything. I wonder if this is how people like Tristan feel all the time? Before I fully stand for my next turn, Jade looks at me and says "Are you okay? You look...different than before." By this point I'm so focused, I can barely register what she's saying, I roll another strike. By the end of the game, I brought my team all the way back, to the point where if I knock over just 3 of the pins, we would win the game. It's my turn now, and I glance over at Tristan and Mackenzie, for the first time all night, his smile was missing. There is a slightly anxious expression on his face. He's seemingly unable to mask his competitive spirit any longer.

Right before I go over to get my ball, Jade gently touches my wrist. "Good luck, you got this." She says with a slight smile. Suddenly I'm brought back to earth. At this point I realize she's sitting considerably closer than she was at the beginning. We're now almost as close as Tristan and Mackenzie are. When did that happen? I go up to roll, trying to refocus myself. The ball leaves my fingers, and immediately veers off to the left. Gutter ball. I lose again.

We leave the bowling alley and step into the warm summer night to head to our cars to leave. The sky is clear and it feels pretty great outside. I guess I should feel happy, the date is over and I got out relatively unscathed, but I definitely blew my opportunity for redemption. There was a moment where I thought maybe she was starting to come around on me, but surely any chances I had with her were extinguished after I folded under pressure, and made a complete fool of myself. Ultimately the night was a failure, but I can take solace in the fact that I'll probably never see Jade again. I'll just have to wipe this date from my memory.

We're almost at our cars, and we're saying our goodbyes when inexplicably Jade says "I'm feeling kind of hungry. Do y'all want to get some food?" It seems like she's asking the group, but she's looking at me while she's asking. Surely she's just trying to finesse me out of a free meal, right? No way she's actually interested in spending more time with me. But maybe she is. I can't let this opportunity go to waste, it's not like I have anything to lose. I guess the double date isn't over yet.

We decided to go to a sushi spot. The four of us are sitting together in a booth. The dim lighting, and indie music sets a cool ambiance. By this point it seems like Jade is having a nice time, she's barely looking at her phone, and her body language is significantly less hostile towards me. I don't know how we got to this point, but I find that I'm enjoying myself too. I find out that Mackenzie and Jade go to one of the local colleges and have only known each other for a few months. Jade moved here from New York and still doesn't really know a lot of people. I find that Jade seems to be somewhat of a free spirit. Often moving from place to place. It makes me wonder what her potential arrival into my life could signify.

"So how did you guys meet?" Jade asks. I get ready to tell her the basic backstory, about how we met playing on the same basketball team at recess in third grade. But before I could say anything, Tristan answered. "In third grade, I just moved to the school, and I didn't know anybody. I got picked on a lot because I was always alone," Tristan says while quickly glancing at me. "One day at recess they were picking teams for basketball, and they were trying to leave me out. Roman insisted I play even though he didn't even know me." I start to fidget with my sushi roll, suddenly unsure what to do with my hands. "That's the day I knew we were meant to be best friends," says Tristan. "Even as kids, Roman was always willing to do the right thing. He's very genuine and there's no one I respect more."

I feel my face grow hot as everyone's eyes shift to me. I've always been terrible at receiving compliments and being the center of attention, so I feel slightly uncomfortable. All these years, and I had no idea, that day at recess had such an impact on Tristan. I've always kind of looked up to him, so it's surreal to hear him say those things about me. I often wondered how we were able to remain close even though our social statuses were so different. At that moment, I'm filled with an overwhelming feeling of gratitude for my friendship with Tristan. While I sit there processing what I'd just heard I glance over at Jade, and see she's looking back at me with a look that almost looks like admiration. I look down at my plate not knowing how to react.

As we're leaving the restaurant, things feel different than before. All of the tension from the beginning of the night has evaporated. Mackenzie and Tristan are looking very cozy together, which was to be expected. What wasn't expected, however, was the way things played out with Jade and I. I went into the night expecting nothing, and then expecting even less than nothing once I saw Jade was my date. Somehow my expectations were completely subverted. Even if I never see her again, I can honestly say I had a pleasant time.

Now we're at our cars, and we say our goodbyes again. This time no one offers up any more moves for the night. Before I go to get into Tristan's car, Jade comes over.

"Here's my number. You should text me sometime," she says with a smile.

THE PRACTICE DATE

"So she gave you her number at the end of the night?"

It's Monday, a couple of days after the double date. I'm at work, still on an emotional high, Camryn and I are discussing how it played out.

"Yeah, we've been texting back and forth all weekend, but I'm thinking I should randomly ghost her to get my revenge."

Camryn shoots me a look, apparently not finding my joke very amusing.

"Yeah yeah, I'm kidding I'm kidding."

A few minutes ago Camryn was telling me about the resort trip with her boyfriend. They have a long distance relationship and don't see each other often. I can tell it means a lot to Camryn that she got to see him this weekend. Whenever she brings him up, she talks so affectionately about him. You can see her practically glowing as she recalls the events that take place. I'm jealous of that kind of connection. Sometimes I wonder if I'll ever have what they have.

For a few minutes, I'm able to zone out and focus on the work at hand. Sorting through clothes, loading up the trash cart to take out to the truck. Simple, easy work. Relationships aren't like that. It's hard being single. Any time I feel like I'm getting somewhere with someone, it ends abruptly. Every new "talking" stage is like a new puzzle that's impossible to solve, but still somehow monotonous. You meet someone, you ask the same boring questions, if you're lucky you actually go on a date, and then things usually fall apart shortly after that.

That's probably why I feel so anxious about how things are going with Jade. While things have been going well the past couple days, I'm getting to the point now where I have to ask her on an official date. This is the same point that she stopped responding last time. How should I ask her? Where should I take her? I might as well be trying to figure out the da vinci code.

"So where are you thinking of taking her for your first date?" asks Camryn.

"I don't know, honestly I'm pretty bad at picking out dating spots," I reply ashamed at my lack of dating expertise.

I'm the kind of person that likes to know a lot about a lot of stuff. It's weird for me to be in positions where I know so little. It makes me feel uncomfortable, vulnerable, and just weak. I want to date people, I want to be good at dating, but it's hard wanting to do something that you've been shown you're not good at. Like that one guy in high school who tries out for the basketball team every year and never makes it. Sometimes I wish I could go to a doctor and get my will to date people surgically removed.

I think life would be easier if I was clairvoyant, or if I could read minds. So then I could just know what to do. I like to think that these trials and tribulations are molding me into the person I'm meant to be, but part of me wishes I could just skip to the end to the point where I'm already a master.

What is life without love? To me love is the meaning of life. We live on a floating rock where everyone has different ideologies about religion and reality. Some say we're living in a simulation, maybe they're right, but the one thing that's important to everyone is love. Love with friendships, love with relationships, love with family. Nothing's more real than that to me. So maybe that's why the idea that I could be so bad at dating is so concerning to me. Am I really living if I can't find somebody to love?

"I think you should take her to have a picnic at Davie's park," Camryn says, snapping me back to reality. "We can go together actually, after work tomorrow. It'd be good practice."

I give her a look, momentarily unsure how to respond. On the surface it seems like she's asking me out, but I know she's in a relationship. Normally if a girl asked me to go on a picnic, I would instantly feel anxious, nervous, uncertain. Thinking of ways for me to not screw it up somehow. At this point I'd say we're work friends. We talk at work, we like each other to an extent, but I wouldn't necessarily classify us as actual friends who hang out and do things outside of work. Normally if a coworker asked me to do something with them after work, even if they're a work friend, I would instantly say no. Why would I want to see them outside of work? Even though those thoughts were going through my mind, this feels different. It doesn't feel like some girl asking me out, or a coworker asking to hang out. It feels chill, natural, like Tristan asking me to go to the movies. Going with her feels like the right choice.

We get to Davie's park, and I'm blown away by how beautiful it is. There's a big, green field of grass surrounded by luscious trees and greenery. There are various walking paths, some of which lead to a bridge over a lake that glitters like diamonds in the sunlight. The sky is a rich shade of blue, and while it's hotter than I'd like, it's still undoubtedly a nice day.

We lay out the spread. We have a variety of fruits, chips, and mini sandwiches. "Slide" by Calvin Harris is playing over the bluetooth speaker I brought from home. Camryn's wearing a tank top and jean shorts. She looks good, Camryn is undeniably attractive, but for some reason it feels as if there's a barrier or some kind of disconnect in my brain that doesn't allow me to view her as a potential love interest. I've only ever seen her at work, so I wasn't sure what it'd be like hanging out with her outside of that setting. The normal critical disposition I've come to expect from Camryn at work, is gone. There's no pressure, it feels like a chill meeting between friends. Even though I've only known her a short time, I feel at ease around her.

"So how are you feeling about your date with Jade?"

"Kind of nervous, I really don't want to mess things up. I'm always paranoid that I'll meet 'the one' but somehow mess it up and be forced to be alone forever."

Camryn laughs. "That's silly to me. What good could possibly come from putting that much pressure on yourself to make things work? If things work out that's great, but if they don't there's always someone else, you know what I mean?"

"See, the thing is in my heart I know you're right, but my head keeps giving me these negative thoughts," I say with a shrug. Sometimes I worry that I'll never overcome my overthinking.

So far the picnic with Camryn is going well. I can already picture taking Jade here for our first date, but I know things will feel differently once I'm with someone I'm actually trying to impress. Especially someone like Jade who I've already built up and idealized in my head.

"How did you know your boyfriend was the one for you?" I ask

"I wouldn't necessarily say he's the one," replies Camryn as she takes a bite of one of the sandwiches.

"So you don't believe in having one person you're destined to be with?"

"Relationships take a lot of work, and they can change very quickly. So I try to take things one day at a time. I don't put a lot of thought into whether he's the one for me or not."

I often imagine what it'd be like to meet my person. We'd see each other from across a crowded room, make our way over to each other, and then boom, love at first sight. Easy. Simple. But real life isn't easy, or simple. Maybe instead of going into my relationships with lofty expectations, I should just try to stay in the moment and enjoy the time I have with the person.

"You know, I'm actually transferring to your school in the fall," says Camryn.

"Really? I had no idea," I responded, genuinely surprised.

"Yeah, once I got my soccer scholarship revoked I knew it was time for a change. I wanted to go somewhere out of state," she replies.

"Are you sure you're not just stalking me?" I ask jokingly.

"Ha, you wish," Camryn responds sarcastically. "Before your first day, Tina told me what school you went to and I was hoping you were cool so I'd have a friend there."

"So my undeniable charm, and award worthy donation sorting skills won you over?" I ask with a slight grin.

"Just be glad I'm your partner, you're still the slowest sorter there. But yes, you have your rare moments where you're not totally insufferable," Camryn admits begrudgingly.

My closed off nature often impedes on my ability to make friends. Up to this point, Tristan is the only person I had who I felt I could open up to. Most times I don't trust people enough to open up and show my true self, so I put up barriers as a form of self protection. In the past, when I'd go to work, I'd listen to my music, and stick to myself, but since working at the thrift shop, Camryn has made an effort to get to know me. She's forced her way through my barriers, and revealed herself to be trustworthy. At the end of the picnic, I have a newfound appreciation for

Camryn. It feels like we've become actual friends, not just work friends.

The next day at work flies by, and before I know it, it's time for me to get ready for my date. The practice date went well, I have a fresh haircut, and before I left work today, Camryn gave me a pep talk. So I'm feeling pretty good. I tediously comb through my wardrobe to look for the perfect fit. After several minutes of trying on various clothing items, I finally found a good combination. Everything's coming together, and the scenery at Davie's park is going to close the deal on what should be a great first date. As I'm changing into my clothes, I hear a loud clap of thunder accompanied by the sound of rain drops falling from the sky. I can't believe my luck.

THE CHANGE-UP

The sky that had just a few minutes ago been a deep shade of blue, is now almost pitch black as the rain continuously pounds the earth. I observe the scene unfolding around me as I ride to Tristan's house. In 30 minutes I'll be using Tristan's car to pick up Jade for our date. What was once a promising evening at the park, has taken a 180, and is now looking as cloudy and bleak as the sky above. My mind is racing. Davie's park seemed like a great spot, and after having the practice date there, I was comfortable there. I had it all planned out in my head. Now I have to start all over. I only have 30 minutes to salvage the date, and this time I don't have Camryn with me to give me ideas.

"Maybe you should just try to reschedule," says Tristan.

"I really feel like it has to be tonight."

I may not know where we're going yet, but I know with absolute certainty that it's now or never for me and Jade. I know how this story goes, I postpone now and the date just keeps getting postponed and ends up never happening. I can't have that. This feels like a landmark moment for me, up to this point I haven't gone on a lot of solo dates, and I didn't want to miss out on this opportunity. Plus, given our history, it's kind of a minor miracle that I'm this close to going on a date with Jade to begin with. Postponing isn't an option.

"How about Marcello's?"

I'd been to Marcello's a couple of times. It's a nice Italian restaurant, a great place for a date, but there was one major issue.

"You know that's like an hour away right? Seems like it's too far for me to be taking your car."

"I know how much this date means to you. Just think of me as Chris Paul giving you an assist."

With other people this kind of thing would make me uncomfortable. I hate when people do favors for me, because it always makes me feel indebted to them. It's different with Tristan. Maybe that's just because I already feel indebted to him. I don't know how I can possibly thank him enough. I wouldn't be where I am with Jade without him. The fact that I have his belief, and support in a situation like this, where I feel so uncertain, fills me with confidence. I refuse to let his belief in me go to waste.

I pull into the parking space outside of Jade's apartment to pick her up. I'm almost shaking with anticipation as I wait for her to come out. The butterflies in my stomach are flying around like it's the first day of spring, and they've just been freed from their cocoons. I can feel my palms start to sweat as I tightly grip the wheel. What if the date is a disaster? On the double date, I had Tristan there to help take the pressure off. This time it's just me and her. What if she decides that I'm not worth her time and ghosts me again? Rejection always stings more when the person meets you in real life. Someone taking the time to meet you, get to know you, and then say "yeah I'm good." It's an experience I'm intimately familiar with, but maybe this time will be different. Just as the tension and anxiety was becoming unbearable, I see the door to the apartment building open, and she walks out.

Despite the rain, she moves with confidence. Her faux locs are styled into a bun, with a couple of strands hanging down both sides of her face. She's holding an umbrella, and wearing fashionable brown leather pants with a black top that perfectly clings to her body. She's wearing dark lipstick that reminds me of Nia Long in the 90s. She's undeniably pretty, and she carries herself like a woman who's been told that countless times. As she gets closer to the car I feel my heartbeat reverberating throughout my body.

"You look really pretty," I say as I clumsily go to open the car door for her.

"Thank you," she says with a smile as she goes to get in.

I still feel nervous as I get back in the car to drive. All day I've been thinking about the perfect songs to play on the drive over. I decide to start safe and play some Drake. The opening to "Passionfruit" serenades us as we pull out of her apartment complex.

"You're not one of those people who hates Drake, and thinks he's overrated, right?" I ask as the car pushes forward through the murky, rainy, night.

"I love him. Personally I think Views is an underrated album."

I glance over and see that she's moving along with the rhythm of the song. I'm way too self conscious to dance in front of other people, but she looks completely at ease, losing herself in the music, despite the limited room she has in the car.

"What would you have done if I said I didn't like Drake?"

"I would have turned the car around and taken you back home," I say with a slight grin on my face.

She laughs softly, "That's the right answer, no Drake slander should be tolerated."

Jade has a slight northern accent. For a guy like me, who's lived in the south his whole life, this makes her seem unique, almost exotic. Something about her seems different from other girls I've come across.

We pull up to the restaurant, and by this point thankfully the rain has stopped. I feel slightly exhilarated when we get inside, and I ask for a table for two for the first time in my life. People glance at us as we walk through the restaurant to our table. For so long I was one of those people. Longingly watching from the side as people around me were going on actual dates. Now that I'm on the other side, it feels good. Like I crossed a forbidden barrier into the VIP section of life. Maybe this is what it feels like to be a main character.

"So how do you like it here compared to where you were in New York?" I ask.

"It's nice, it's smaller than I thought it'd be, but it's nice for now."

"I like coming back here during the summer. I'm not sure if I want to move back after I graduate," I reply as I go to take a sip of my root beer.

"I like traveling, and I want to live in a lot of different places. I don't plan on living here long once I finish school," Jade says self assuredly.

I've often fantasized about moving across the country and starting a new life where I don't know anybody. It seems far-fetched, the only reason I had the courage to go to a college that's hours away from home is because Tristan was there with me. It's hard enough making friends and getting out of the house now, I can only imagine how much harder it would be in a place where I don't know anybody. I prefer stability in my life, and Jade's constantly changing lifestyle is completely foreign to me.

"Committing to things is hard for me. Whether it's a person, a place, a job, it's hard," says Jade.

"Is that why you ghosted me when we first started talking?"

The question leaves my mouth as if it's a prisoner trying to make a jailbreak. For the past few days I'd been trying to erase the question from my brain. Afraid that me bringing it up would serve as a reminder that she ghosted me before and cause her to ghost me again. That fear has made me feel like I'm walking on a tightrope dozens of feet in the air, but the question has been haunting me ever since she gave me her number at the end of our double date. It was the elephant in the room, the inevitable obstacle to our budding relationship. The question is out there now, no way to take it back. I'm sure that I need to know the answer if I have any hope at all of moving forward with her.

"Honestly, yes. I felt like things were moving too fast, and I wasn't ready."

"What changed your mind?"

Jade takes a moment to consider this question, as if unsure herself why she was there with me. The lighting in the restaurant is soft, and there's a candle gently flickering in the middle of the table. The candlelight makes her face look otherworldly as she casually ponders the question.

"The double date with Mackenzie and Tristan. It felt like the universe was giving me a sign to give you another chance. When we were bowling, you radiated this quiet confidence that I thought was cool. I figured I might as well see what an actual date with you would be like."

"How am I doing so far?"

Jade laughs softly "I'll let you know once I taste this food."

Whether it's God or the universe, I often think about the role they play in my day to day life. I'm not religious, and I generally like to believe that God doesn't have a major say in most things in life, but it's hard to imagine there was no divine intervention involved in my relationship with Jade.

Our food comes to the table. Jade gets the shrimp scampi, and I get lasagna. After the first bite, I feel instant relief. Nothing helps relieve tension and nerves as much as a good meal.

"How do you like your food?" I ask as I take another bite of food.

"It's good. It makes me want to visit Italy."

"Why's that?" I ask with a mouthful of lasagna.

"Haven't you ever tasted ethnic food and wanted to see what it was like if it was made in the country it originates from?"

I take another bite of food as I consider the question. As much as I like the lasagna, I don't think it's making me want to go to Italy. "I've never really thought about it like that honestly."

"All I want in life is to travel the world, see cool things, and try good food," says Jade.

As someone who's reserved with a somewhat conservative approach to life, someone like Jade is like a shock to the system. I find it interesting the way she speaks so definitively, as if her fate is already decided. I've never met anyone like her and I can feel myself becoming more and more drawn to her uniqueness.

I pulled up to her house after the dinner feeling pretty good. Tristan's car is in one piece and the dinner was less awkward than I thought it'd be.

"Thank you for dinner. I had a really nice time!" Jade is smiling, but her voice is hard to read.

"Can I walk you to your door?"

Jade gives a soft chuckle "Yeah, okay."

As we're walking to her door, I feel the nerves from earlier in the night resurface. I'm unsure what I should do now. I briefly imagine a scene from the movie *Hitch* when Will Smith's character is explaining the 90/10 rule for kissing to Kevin James' character. In the movie, despite his awkward and meek nature, Kevin James' character had the guts to go for it when the time came. My time is coming soon too, but am I ready for it? I know if I were Tristan, I would kiss Jade without a second thought. But I'm not Tristan. I've never even kissed a girl before.

We get to Jade's door and there's a moment of awkward silence as we both try to figure out the next move. She looks at me expectantly. We're so close that her citrusy perfume threatens to overwhelm and intoxicate me. For a second I'm focused on her lips. They're the perfect size, the dark shade of lipstick perfectly complimenting the rest of her face, acting almost like a magnet drawing me in. I'm mesmerized. Without thinking I go to make my move, slowly, but decisively I go in. I'm so close now that I can smell the peppermint gum that she's been chewing through-out the night. Centimeters away now, so close I can almost feel it. I notice her moving in slightly too. Right before our lips touch, I move my head to the side slightly, and wrap my arms around her, giving her the most awkward hug of all time.

"We should do this again sometime," I say as I feel my face turning bright red with embarrassment.

Jade studies my face intently, as if trying to get into my head. I expect her to look disappointed in my inability to go all the way. Or maybe even relieved that she didn't have to kiss someone she wasn't really that into. But her facial expression doesn't display any disappointment or relief like I thought it might. It's more like curiosity. Like the look a cat gets when it gets a new toy.

"Yeah, for sure. I'll let you know my schedule. Text me when you get home." Jade gives me one last smile before she heads inside.

THE MOVIES

"I just think you're overreacting," says Camryn.

It's almost a week later, and I'm at work. I'm talking to Camryn, recounting what took place on my date with Jade.

"Everytime I feel like I've made progress, I'm reminded of how little I've made."

Camryn sighs, "have you talked to her about the date? Like to see where you stand?"

"We're supposed to go out again, but I don't know, things are weird."

"What do you mean?"

The truth is that while we have a date planned, and it's not even really planned it's just something I mentioned to her, Jade has been far from active when it comes to responding to my texts. She frequently goes all day without responding to me. For some reason this seems to make me like her more. I find myself checking my phone several times a day hoping to see her name appear on the screen.

"I just think she's less invested than I am."

"That's okay. Everyone needs to move at their own pace, you know what I mean?"

I know Camryn's right, but I can't shake the feeling that the awkward hug at the end of the night, set me back with Jade. I feel a similar sensation to when I approached that mystery girl on campus the last day before summer break. A deep, burning disappointment that threatens to completely engulf me. Have I really grown so little since that moment?

"I just don't know what I'm supposed to do. Should I keep texting her? Should I let her make the next move? I just don't know," I responded, clearly exasperated. My lack of experience never fails to make things more difficult for me. Is this the stress that all men feel when dealing with women?

"Blowing up her phone is probably the worst thing you can do," says Camryn pointedly, as she starts sorting through another bag of donations. "You gotta play it cool. Just try to take your mind off of her for a while."

After work, as usual, I make my way to the gym. While most people I know would classify me as calm, cool, and collected, when it comes to women I am none of those things. Hopefully this workout helps take my mind off things.

My breathing is extremely heavy and labored as I struggle my way through my workout. My arms are drenched with sweat as I continuously rep my way through each exercise. For the first time all day, my head is clear. Even a chronic overthinker like my-self has trouble thinking about women when I'm gasping for air during my workouts. There's something so beautiful to me about exercise. There's beauty in the struggle to better yourself. The gym is like the antithesis to my actual life. In the gym, I feel free, I'm completely self assured, and at ease. The sweat and effort I put in leads me closer to my goal. The awkwardness and discom-fort I endure in the gym leads to growth and improvement. That same awkwardness and discomfort in my real life, like the end of the date with Jade, just seems to lead to pain.

I get home to get ready to go to the movies. During the summer, the movie theater up the street has $5 movie showings on tuesdays. Tristan and I have made it a tradition to go every week. This week we're watching the new *Uncle Drew* movie which I'm excited about. In high school, Tristan and I used to watch the *Uncle Drew* videos together when they were released on YouTube. Uncle Drew is the basketball player, Kyrie Irving, who goes around to different basketball courts and destroys people, while disguised as an old man. It should be a chill way to get my mind off of Jade for a couple of hours.

The aroma of popcorn hits us as soon as we walk into the movie theater. It's a warm, inviting scent that I've grown to love over the years. Going to the movies has become one of my favorite pastimes. For a couple of hours I can escape into the movie. I can watch the protagonist get their happy ending and fantasize that I'm the one getting a happy ending too.

"Hold on, I'm gonna take a leak right quick," says Tristan before heading to the bathroom.

As I wait for him in the hallway outside of the bathroom, I catch a glimpse of someone familiar out of the corner of my eye. I turn to look, careful not to bring attention to myself. This time I have a clear look. Standing in line by the concessions stand, is a woman who's around my age. She's pretty with faux locs and rich brown skin. The recognition slams into me like a blindside hit from Ray Lewis. There's no doubt that the woman is Jade, the same person who's been ignoring my texts all day.

For a second a small part of me thinks that maybe it could be her sister, or just someone who looks a lot like her, but no, I'm sure it's her. She's not there alone either, there's a guy there with her. I briefly consider the fact that they could just be friends. After all, I went on a practice date with Camryn just last week, so it's not totally out of the question. But that idea is quickly nixed from my mind as I take in the whole scene. Jade has a full face of makeup and is dressed to impress, it's clear they're on a date. The expression on his face, the look in his eyes, is similar to the one I must have had just a few days earlier. The worst part of the whole scene is that I can see she's on her phone. It's like a visual affirmation that she's ignoring me.

I feel so many emotions bubbling inside, threatening to erupt. There's a cold stabbing pain in my chest and stomach as I try to process what I've seen. I think about how I felt a few days ago when I was with Jade. I felt proud, on top of the world. Now that guy gets to feel that way instead of me. I feel the jealousy and animosity building up inside. Why couldn't she just text me saying she wasn't interested? Most of all I feel embarrassed. How silly I must be to think I actually had a chance. I may as well have said I wanted to enroll in Hogwarts to become a wizard.

Tristan gets out of the bathroom, and we walk to our theater. I feel a haze clouding over the optimism I was feeling just a few minutes ago. The movie goes by in a blur. Normally I enjoy breaking down the movie while I watch, looking for the hidden messages and critiquing the storylines. But tonight I can't seem to concentrate at all. The *Uncle Drew* movie should be a relatively easy film to digest, but it may as well have been in Japanese considering how much of it I actually took in. I find myself longing to fade into the darkness of the theater to try to find a way to escape the pain I'm feeling.

Tristan loves sports, especially basketball so naturally he's a big fan of the movie. As we walk outside to his car he's cheerfully recounting his favorite scenes. While he's going on about the movie, I feel as if I'm in the upside down world from *Stranger Things*, face to face with a demogorgon. Tristan glances over at me as if noticing something's off.

"What's wrong, Rome?" My facial expression must be pretty troubling, because he sounds legitimately worried.

"You'll never guess who I saw in the theater," I say as we get close to Tristan's car.

"Who?" Tristan asks as he opens his car door to get in.

"Jade. And she was there with some guy. I'm blown."

"Man, that's tough."

"Yeah, our date ended kind of awkwardly the other day, but I don't know."

I take a moment to gather my thoughts. I can tell I feel strongly about what's happened, but I only went on one date with Jade. As much as I liked her, it doesn't make sense for me to feel as invested as I do after only one date. I can feel myself trying to hold back my true feelings from Tristan. This would only seem like a small setback to a guy like him, it's hard for me to imagine he would understand why I feel so devastated.

"I just feel kind of silly. I thought we had a decent connection."

The rest of the drive goes by without any conversation. The sound of Frank Ocean's haunting voice washes over us and fills the car as we make our way back home. I stare out the window despondently, trying not to feel like a failure. We pull up to my house, but before I can get out Tristan stops me.

"Do you remember Liz? The girl I was seeing for a little while freshman year?"

Liz was the first girl Tristan got with freshman year. I saw them together for a few weeks but it seemed like things ended abruptly.

"Yeah I remember her, why?"

Tristan takes a deep breath. "I never told you this because I was ashamed." His eyes are focused on his steering wheel. "The reason we stopped talking is because I saw her out with another guy."

For a moment there's silence, I don't know how to respond. I didn't think Tristan ever experienced anything like that.

"Wow I had no idea," I say, genuinely surprised. "I just figured you lost interest."

"Yeah, no, if anything she lost interest in me," Tristan says with a sarcastic and somewhat bitter laugh. "She told me that since we weren't exclusive, she was going to explore her options. At the time I didn't understand that that's how dating worked, and I wasn't ready for it."

The more he talked about it, the more it sounds exactly like my situation with Jade.

"I guess I'm just trying to say that we've all been there. The best thing you can do is try to enjoy dating for what it is and not take things too seriously. I don't want you to feel discouraged."

I try to digest everything he said. "It all just seems so complicated. I wish things were simpler."

"Dating can be annoying, but it can be fun too. You'll see," Tristan says with a grin.

"I can't believe she would do that."

The next day at work, I tell Camryn about seeing Jade at the movies the night before. Camryn is a serial monogamous, so the idea that someone could go on a date with someone just days after going on a date with someone else was completely foreign. I appreciated her concern, but after the talk with Tristan, I decided to just charge it to the game. It still stings, but it is what it is.

I tried to get into the dating game, I really did, but maybe it just isn't for me. I gave it my best shot, but maybe I'm just not ready yet. The rest of the day goes by smoothly. It's mid July now, and the summer is more than halfway over. Even though things didn't work out with Jade, it makes me feel somewhat satisfied knowing that I'm close to the goal amount I wanted to save to buy a car. As I'm walking up the stairs to my room, I feel my phone buzz. It's a text from Jade. "Do you still want to go on that picnic?"

THE PARK PT. 2

My fingers move around the video game controller as I frantically try to perfectly maneuver the players on my team. I don't have work today, and I've spent the day playing NBA 2K at Tristan's house. I've yet to win a game against him all day.

"So have you responded to Jade yet?" Tristan asks as one of his players hits a 3-point shot.

Tristan is of course referring to the text that Jade sent me the night before. I've been trying to play it cool, but I've been thinking about the text way more than I'd like to admit. I've been trying not to seem too eager, but the only reason I've been able to hold out as long as I have is because I truly don't know how to respond.

"I'm not sure. What do you think I should do?"

"Well that depends. How do you feel about her?"

I think back to the dinner date I had with Jade. I remember how good it felt to be there with her. How cool and unique she seemed to me. Secretly I had been fantasizing about what being with her would be like. Getting to feel the way I felt during our date all the time. She'd probably introduce me to a whole new world of things that I'd never tried before. The idea of having someone I could be intimate with, someone I could try new things with, seemed too good to be true. I feel like one of those birds who tries to fly into people's houses, looking for a free snack, but actually flies head first into a glass door. I feel like a wrestler, scaling to the top of a ladder in a ladder match, reaching up for the championship belt before inevitably getting pushed off.

I've been playing sports for as long as I can remember. I love competition, I live for it. But I never thought I would have to deal with competition when it came to the dating scene. I think back to all the times in high school, and so far in college, when someone swoops in and takes a girl that I was interested in. I feel powerless to stop it. Naturally a good woman would have a lot of other suitors, but I always figured that once we got to the actual dating part, all that would cease. It always looks so easy in the movies. Boy meets girl, and they fall in love. Why does life always feel the need to complicate things? The thought of competing with guys like Tristan for women seems almost impossible. I might as well be asked to beat LeBron James one on one with one arm tied behind my back.

"I don't know, I just feel like if she liked me, things wouldn't be like this. You know what I mean?" I reply, while one of my players gets blocked by one of Tristan's players.

"Well she asked you to go out again, that's got to count for something, right?"

For the next few minutes while we play 2K, you can hear nothing except the sounds of buttons rapidly being pressed, and the music playing over the bluetooth speaker.

"How are things with you and Mackenzie?" I ask, breaking the silence, hoping for a more positive turn in the conversation. Mackenzie, the tall, pretty blonde girl that we went bowling with. They looked like they were having a good time together, and she was definitely Tristan's type. Maybe Tristan will have a relationship with a girl that's more than just a short fling, for once.

"You know how it goes. On to the next," says Tristan. The disappointment in his voice is extremely apparent. "I'm kind of jealous of you in some ways. I lose interest in girls so fast, I don't know if I'll ever be able to commit."

For years, Tristan has been able to get basically any girl he wanted. I never considered that that could get tiring. It feels to me like whenever a rich person tells a poor person that money isn't everything. A statement that, while true, is completely beyond my current level of understanding.

"Ever since I met Liz, my relationship with women has felt empty, hollow, and unfulfilling."

For the first time I can see the frustration that has seemingly been bubbling under the surface this whole time. For Tristan it must feel like he's trying a bunch of different flavors of ice cream, but not liking any of them, except the one that's now out of stock. I wish I could think of something profound to say to magically solve all of his problems, but the words are escaping me. I can only imagine the despair he must feel, believing that his one shot at true happiness has already slipped through his fingers. Would it be worse for me to feel regret with Jade the way Tristan does with Liz? Or is it worse to get completely and utterly rejected the way I have so often in the past?

"I think I'm going to text Jade back," I mutter with uncertainty.

It's a few days later, and I'm at Davie's park with Jade. The bright, summer sun beams down on us as we casually eat and converse on a picnic blanket. We have a nice spread complete with ham and cheese subs, an assortment of fruit, chips, and lemonade. It's a warm day, but not to the point that it's uncomfortable. Jade is wearing a baby blue sundress, and the sun radiates off of her brown skin, making it look like she's glowing. Her perfect white teeth shimmer in the sunlight. The sweet scent of strawberries hangs heavily in the air, as Jade reaches into the bag to grab some to make a fruit salad for herself.

"I'm really glad that we don't have to go on this date in the middle of a hurricane like the last time," says Jade with a sly grin on her face.

"Yeah I bribed the guy working the weather machine to make sure it was nice out today."

Jade smiles slightly and laughs pleasantly in response.

It seems like we're both more comfortable with each other now that we got the first date out of the way, but I'm still feeling a little tense. I wonder how I'm doing compared to the guy she was with the other night? Did she smile and laugh at his jokes too?

After the first date, I constantly thought about what our potential future would be like. The dates we'd go on, the gifts we'd get each other for Valentine's day, and other holidays. It was all crystal clear to me at the time, but once I saw her on a date with someone else, it's like all of that started to evaporate in my mind. When you meet someone new it's hard to imagine how things will end between you, so in the beginning it's easy for me to see myself being with someone long term. Once the first obstacle gets introduced that could potentially end the budding relationship, it brings me back to reality. Now, instead of fantasizing about my future with Jade, I find myself comparing myself to these phantom men who I've never met, in an attempt to prepare myself for the inevitable.

"This is my second time here actually. I came here with a friend of mine to practice for my date with you," I say, suddenly realizing how weird that must sound.

"Oh, that's nice," replied Jade, sounding unfazed while taking out her phone to take a video of the park and the food layout.

Despite how apathetic she seems, I feel kind of guilty. I saw her at the movies with another guy, and somehow I'm the one feeling guilty about coming here with a friend. I feel like one of those men in the old Batman movie that get hypnotized by Poison Ivy's love potion.

"She was just a friend though, it wasn't like a romantic thing," I quickly and awkwardly added.

"It's okay for you to see other people. We're not together like that."

Her words strike me like a sharp blade. I feel like one of the henchmen in Kill Bill who have to face Uma Thurman's character. Hopelessly outmatched and ultimately doomed to die a gruesome death. The worst part is that I'm not even caught off guard by what she said. Tristan and I talked in depth about a similar situation he had, and I literally saw her out with another guy. And yet...and yet, it still hurts. Just a few days ago, I was googling how many dates it takes before you can make things official, and now this feels like the deathblow to whatever potential relationship was forming. Before I can continue fantasizing about excruciating deaths that I think accurately portray how I'm feeling, I'm interrupted by Jade.

"Honestly I just feel like dating multiple people helps to show you what you like and don't like in a partner. If it's meant to be with someone it'll work out."

Okay, maybe I overreacted a little bit. This doesn't seem to be the deathblow that I thought it was a second ago. It's not like I disagree, Jade is obviously right. It's good to have options to see what works best for you, but the problem is I don't have any other options, and I've already decided that I want to be with her. But then maybe I'm only so pressed to be with her because I don't have other options. I really hate how my insecurities have such an effect on my thought process like this.

I briefly put these thoughts aside. "Do you think you could ever be in a monogamous relationship?"

"Maybe down the line, but I'm mainly interested in meeting new people for now."

I find this answer interesting. I'm dating people to find "the one", to find stability. Jade is driven by an endless curiosity that I don't know if I'll ever fully understand. On paper it seems like a bad match, but I'm determined to be the one that can satisfy her curiosities.

"So how do I stack up against the other people you've been seeing?" I ask, partially hoping she just laughs it off and doesn't actually answer.

"Well, right now I'd say you're in first place, but don't get too comfortable, I change my mind quickly," says Jade with a slight smile on her face.

Davie's park has a walking trail that snakes through the park into a woodsy area that Jade and I are walking on. Our date has lasted around an hour and a half, and is starting to wind down. We pause briefly by a pond, to admire the radiant sunset on the horizon. It's a dazzling mix of yellow, crimson, and orange. Like something out of a movie. It looks like one of those pictures you see on Instagram that you think must have a filter, but this is even better because it's real life. The woods are behind us, and there's no one around. All you can hear are the occasional crickets chirping, and frogs croaking.

There's an incredible stillness in the air. I feel extremely tranquil, and mellow. This is my moment, I decide. This is my moment to make up for the awkward hug from the first date. This epiphany hits me the way it would if I was deciding what I should make for dinner. It doesn't feel like a huge groundbreaking moment for me. There's no celebratory fireworks. It just feels like it's time. I gently wrap my arm around Jade's waist and go in, slowly, but deliberately.

Her lips are soft and inviting, like a warm blanket fresh out of the dryer on a cold, snowy day. When our tongues intertwined, it was a weird sensation, like a weird dance that was happening in our mouths. I could feel her passion, her sensuality, oozing throughout her body. For a few minutes, we continued. Our rhythm is completely in sync. It feels like an eternity, but also like no time has passed. I could live in this moment, I think to myself. Finally we pull apart.

"That was nice," says Jade with a content smile. I reply with incoherent gibberish, as I feel my spirit float away on cloud 9. I can't hide the stupid grin on my face as we walk into the sunset.

THE CAR

It's now early august. It's been a few weeks since the date in the park with Jade. We've gone on a couple more dates since then, but we're not any closer to forming any kind of committed relationship. I've enjoyed myself with her, and part of me thinks I should just leave it at that and not try to pursue things further. After all, the summer's coming to an end, and I'm going back to school soon. The best case scenario would include a long distance relationship which nobody wants. I mean, I don't even have a car...yet.

After a summer of long, grueling work days, I have saved enough to buy a car. All the hoops I would have to go through to go on dates, or even go to mundane places like the gym, it feels good knowing I won't have to deal with it anymore. All the times I've had to ask for a ride, or use someone else's car, or walk, took a toll on me. I think of myself as a fiercely independent person, so having to rely on others for transportation has been frustrating and humbling to say the least. I always felt like the song "No Scrubs" was a little too close to my own situation. Imagine asking a girl out, but you have to ask her for a ride, or having to ask to use someone else's car. Getting a girl to go out with you is hard enough without that built in impediment. I was tired of feeling like a scrub, and now is my chance to change that.

I tried to get a car last summer, but I didn't have enough money, and I didn't have any credit, so financing the car was out of the question. I distinctly remember how optimistic I was at the time. I had gathered all of my pennies and went to the car dealership, ready to spend it all. I saw the car, I test drove the car, I envisioned myself in the car. It felt like it was already mine. I had worked hard that summer for a car too, but I fell short.

"I understand you're anxious to get a car right now, but you can't spend all your money on a car note every month. You need enough money for food, and other necessities," the car salesman had said at the time. In hindsight he was right, but at the time I was extremely dejected. I had already decided that the no car life was not for me, and by that point I was fed up with it. Imagine how ready I am for a car now, a year later. Especially considering I've been dealing with a girl like Jade, who loves to go different places. She's had to pick me up for a couple of our dates, and it just left a bad taste in my mouth. Now, after a year of letting that disappointment stew within me, a year of saving and working, I was ready to move past that carless phase in my life.

My dad drops me off at the dealership. "Good luck, kid. This is a big moment for you, you should be proud," he says before I go to walk in. I already know what car I want, a charcoal gray 2015 Honda Accord. It's not some fancy sports car, but to me it might as well be the newest Lamborghini.

"Roman, good to see you again," booms the boisterous car salesman. He is a large man, with an even larger voice, reminding me of Vince McMahon. He's wearing a blue button down shirt, with gray slacks, and a name tag that says his name is Leroy Armstrong, which is lucky for me because in the year since I saw him last, I had completely forgotten his name. He gets up to shake my hand, and we both sit down. On his desk is a clear shaker bottle with a green top, similar to the ones I see when I go to the gym for people to make protein shakes or mix pre-workout. There's also a picture of him with what I'm guessing is his family, as well as a picture of him at a weight lifting competition.

"So let's get down to it. You wanted to check out the Honda Accord, is that right?" Leroy asks, while maintaining intense eye contact.

"Yes sir, I've had my eye on it for a while now," I reply, feeling the anticipation and anxiety build up inside of me.

Leroy hands me a couple of forms to fill out and sign. "Just fill these out, and we can go for a test drive."

We get outside and I'm immediately overwhelmed by all the cars that are in the lot. We walk through a few rows in the august heat, and then I see it. Gleaming underneath the direct sunlight is the car that I've been fantasizing about for several months. Leroy begins giving me a run down of the car. Telling me the mileage, and the different features that the car has, but that's all basically background noise to me. I've been doing my own research on this car for months, I know it like the back of my hand.

Once we get on the road, I'm reminded of how good it felt a year ago to drive this car. It's incredibly smooth and handles well. It makes me feel like I'm in a Fast and Furious movie.

"This baby has a V6 engine, 185 horsepower, and around 25 miles per gallon," Leroy continues in the background, but I can barely register what he's saying. My mind continues to fantasize about driving Jade around in this car, my car. Nothing impresses women more than loud music, and fast driving. Surely we'll be together now that I have my own car.

We get back to the dealership, and it's time for me to sign all the various contracts and forms necessary for me to buy the car. The car is $12,000, which I'm paying in cash since I still don't have a credit card or any sort of credit history. My parents chipped in to help me pay for it, which I'm thankful for.

Even though my parents are divorced and can't stand the sight of each other,, as their only child, they still come together to help me from time to time if I need it. I admire their ability to support me even though they have such a contentious relationship. I remember all the arguments they had when I was growing up, before finally, mercifully, the divorce came when I was 13. Before that though, the household always felt tense, and on edge. As young as I was, I could feel the resentment between them. That's why I felt so much relief when the divorce happened. It seems like my parents feel the same way too, as they both seem happier now that they're apart. I have a lot of love for both of my parents, but their relationship makes me feel like I may ultimately be doomed in my future relationships. They say we learn a lot about relationships through our parents, and I'm afraid that I've picked up a lot of bad habits that could stop me from finding happiness in the future.

"Well Roman, it's been a pleasure doing business with you," booms Leroy, as he interrupts my train of thought. "If you, or anyone you know, has any car needs in the future, tell 'em to call Leroy Armstrong. I'll get you in your dream car guaranteed," he says as he goes to shake my hand with the strongest grip I've ever felt. Leroy may be a little loud and intense, but I'm grateful for his help. I may even miss the big guy.

As I drive my new car off the lot, I'm hit with an overwhelming feeling of accomplishment and freedom. Is this how birds feel the first time they fly? I can literally go anywhere I want right now. I don't have to ask for permission, or bribe someone with extra gas money, I can just go. My mind immediately jumps to Jade. While we've gone on a few dates at this point, there have been times where I've had to cancel or postpone because I didn't have transportation. Now I don't have to worry about that. Now that I have my own car we can just hang out together whenever we're both free. What a game changer.

Once I get to a red light, I eagerly get out my phone to text Jade. "Guess who has their own car now? Wanna go for a drive with me and get dinner tomorrow?" I feel a huge rush of adrenaline and optimism for the future. Maybe a long distance relationship with Jade would be a good thing. I could drive back to see her every weekend, it'd give us our own independence, which I know she'd like, and it'd give us enough quality time to make it work. The more I think about it, the more I think it's a good idea.

On my way home I stop at the store to buy flowers to give to Jade on our next date. The plan is to give the flowers to her and then propose this "long distance relationship" idea to her. I can't remember the last time I felt so happy or excited about something in my life. A lot of my life seems to end in disappointment. It happens so often that I've almost become numb to it, but being with Jade brings me joy. This just feels right to me.

Jade's Interlude

From a young age, Jade has had to shoulder an incredible amount of responsibility. Her mom died in a car accident when she was 10. As the oldest of four children, she took on a motherly role in her family, watching over her younger siblings while her father worked long hours. Her father who, while very loving, was also very protective over his kids, and the love became almost suffocating once his beloved wife died in an unexpected accident. He became fearful that something similar would happen to one of his kids. He became a recluse, only ever going to work, and doing the occasional unavoidable errand. He forced his kids to follow suit, they were allowed to do very little outside of going to school. This sparked Jade's curiosity. She knew there was more to life than the way she had been living, and she wanted to see it all. She loved her family, but the responsibilities she had to carry at such a young age were a burden. She knew she couldn't become who she was meant to be with such a heavy weight constantly on her shoulders. When it came time to graduate high school, she had been frantically applying to scholarships so she could leave her home, go to school, and be free. Luckily, she earned enough in scholarships to leave. She vowed to herself to not let herself be tied down. She wanted to learn about herself, learn about people, learn about the world, learn about everything. She wanted to live free for as long as she possibly could.

She really liked Roman. He was awkward, genuine, and was different from the guys she usually went out with in a way that made him seem cool to her. But as much as she liked Roman, she didn't like him enough to compromise her freedom. She knew it was time to end things. And that's why, when she saw his text message, she never responded.

THE END OF SUMMER

As I walk down stairs to leave my house for my last day at work, I try to ignore the depressing sight of dying flowers on the kitchen counter. They're the flowers that I was supposed to give to Jade. The flowers that have been sitting out for four days now. It's now the middle of August, a few days after I bought my new car. Jade never responded to the text I sent asking to go to dinner. Or the three subsequent texts I sent afterwards, when I was trying to see what was going on. Or the two minute voicemail I left for her last night. For all I knew she had died in a horrific bear related incident. I actually know she's alive and well, because while she hasn't been talking to me, she's still maintained a consistent stream of posts on her Instagram story. Forget a long distance relationship, I can't even maintain a short distance situationship.

Of course the smart thing to do, would be to throw the flowers away, or at least put them in some water or something. Every time I look at them, it's like a fresh wave of pain washes over me. The wilting flowers serve as a perfect metaphor for my wilting relationship with Jade. But I can't seem to get rid of them. Maybe it's because once I throw them away, I know it's really over, or maybe because I think that I deserve the pain that I feel whenever I see them. This is what I get for trying to get into the dating game. This is what I get for thinking I could actually be happy with a girl as cool, and pretty as Jade.

In my twenty years of life, whenever I'm feeling alone, I always like to think that I'm meant for more. That I'm meant to be with someone who I really like. But how could something be meant for me if it brings me so much pain? The flowers serve as a reminder that I'm not meant for more, and that I should just embrace my loneliness. They're not only a metaphor for my relationship with Jade, but they're a metaphor for how I'm feeling too. Shriveled, weak, pathetic. Maybe this is what I need to crush my romantic ambitions once and for all.

The drive to my job helps to clear my mind a little bit. Hopefully a few hours of mindless work will help to clear it even more.

"It's crazy that the summer's basically over," says Camryn while she tries to fix the cushion on her seat.

"Yeah, I think I'm going to miss this place," I reply.

"Really? Why?"

That's a valid question. I liked the job, it was easy money, but it's not like I'm going to miss all the hot days, and manual labor. I don't even get along all that well with my coworkers. It seemed like they liked me at first, but once they saw that Camryn and I had become friends, they avoided me like the plague.

"You know, I think I'm mostly going to miss all of the passive aggressive glances from my coworkers," I say, jokingly.

"Oh, shut up," Camryn says, with a slight smile on her face.

"I think I'm just not a big fan of change. I've gotten used to the routine of coming here, and going to the gym everyday."

"Soon you'll have a new routine though. A better routine."

"Yeah, but who will be there to give me girl advice every day? You know I'm hopeless," I say while sneaking a pair of black Nike shorts into my bag. It being my last day has made me determined to sneak off with as much usable stuff as possible.

"Hopeless? Please, you've at least advanced beyond that level thanks to me. Plus we'll still get to see each other sometimes, it's not like I won't need friends once I transfer. I literally won't know anyone there."

"Yeah, but it won't be the same," I reply dejectedly.

Deep down I know how things will play out. Once we're not required to see each other every day, we'll slowly lose touch with each other. We'll make an effort to see each other, but then the inevitable will happen. She already has a boyfriend, and as her guy friend, I'm easily replaceable. It probably won't take long until we're not even on speaking terms anymore. This thought makes me sad, but that's how my life has always gone. I've come to accept that with the exception of Tristan, everyone in my life is temporary.

Camryn rolls her eyes. "Don't be so dramatic. You can't get rid of me that easily. Oh, by the way, did Jade ever respond?"

"Yeah she did. As a matter of fact, I'm planning our wedding vows as we speak," I say, my words dripping with sarcasm.

"I'm guessing that's a no. I'm sorry to hear that, I know how much you liked her," Camryn says.

"Yeah, it just sucks. She could've at least texted me, and told me it was over," I say glumly. "Actually, now that I think about it, that would've sucked too. I guess it's not about how it ended, but just the fact that it ended at all."

"Yeah I get that, it's your first real experience with a girl. I remember my first breakup, there's really nothing that can prepare you for it. At least you've gained a little experience now."

I sigh."Yeah, but we weren't even together really. It doesn't even count as a real breakup. It makes me worried about how I'll feel when I experience real heartbreak. I don't know if it's worth it to try to find someone to be with if it leads to this kind of pain. Maybe I'm just not meant to find love."

Camryn looks at me. Her expression that was compassionate just seconds ago, hardens, becoming very serious. "Tristan, don't ever let anyone crush your spirit. You're a good guy. You treated Jade with kindness and respect. Any girl should feel lucky to know you. Don't let this break you, don't give her, or anyone else that satisfaction, ever."

There's a brief pause as I digest what she's said. I can feel myself start to sweat a little bit from the intensity of her words. "Thank you for that," I say, finally.

"If you go through life with that kind of mindset, you'll never meet your person. And everyone deserves to meet their person," she says definitively.

The rest of the shift goes by in a flash. There was no more talk of Jade, or women in general, which I was grateful for. Now it's time for me to leave. Camryn walks outside with me to my car.

"I'm going to miss this place," I say as I look back trying to take a mental picture. I can tell it'll be my last time ever being here.

"That's cool and all, but imagine how I'm going to feel for the next few days. I won't have anyone to talk to," Camryn says. While my last day is today, hers isn't until the end of the week.

"We'll both be moving onto bigger and better things soon enough," I say as I open the driver's side car door. This will be a summer I never forget.

Once I get home, I go straight to the kitchen counter. Camryn's words fill me with the resolve I need to get rid of the flowers, and any remnants of Jade once and for all. Camryn's right, I can't let Jade keep me down. It's time to move on.

It's a few days after my last day at work, and I've been staying with my mom. It's become a tradition for me to spend the last week of the summer at my mom's, which has its pros and cons. When I'm with my dad, I pretty much have free reign. As long as I'm not doing anything illegal, I'm good. My mom isn't exactly strict, but unlike my dad, when I stay with her I'm required to spend time with her. Tonight we went out to Cracker Barrel to get dinner. I don't mind it mostly, but she has a habit of making me feel anxious by bringing up things I'd rather not talk about.

"So, Roman, how do you like your new car?" my mom asks while stabbing at her scrambled eggs. Even though it's dinnertime, it's kind of our thing to get breakfast for dinner on the last day of summer.

"It's nice, I like how it handles. It's made it a lot easier to get around."

"Have you driven any young ladies around in it yet?" she asks, causing me to almost choke on my pancake. This kind of question is her go to, she loves to know all about my love life. That being said, it's also the kind of question I hate the most. Usually I try to make it seem like I have a colorful and thriving love life, instead of the dull lonely one that I actually have, so I don't come off as too much of a loser. This time though, fresh off my summer fling with Jade, I actually have someone interesting to talk about. Unfortunately I'm definitely not willing to bring her up in conversation with my mom. Imagine the disappointment she would feel knowing how unlucky I've been with women.

"Not yet," I respond while trying to maintain an inconspicuous face. "I did meet this cool girl named Camryn though. She was one of my coworkers." Normally I wouldn't bring up Camryn in a conversation like this because we're just friends, and it would lead to awkward follow up questions, but at this point I'd do anything to avoid talking about Jade.

"Hmm, Camryn, do I know her?"

I roll my eyes. "No, mom, why would you know her?" My mom always thinks she knows the people I talk about even though she never does.

"Okay, well is she pretty?"

"Yeah she's pretty cute, but she has a boyfriend" I say before taking a bite of my turkey bacon.

"Oh, well you know it doesn't really count unless there's a ring involved," my mom responds, seemingly oblivious to how wrong that sounds.

"Mom, you can't say stuff like that," I say as I hit my forehead with the palm of my hand out of exasperation.

"That's how I met your father. I was with this other guy, James, but your dad—"

"Okay, mom," I interject before she can get out of hand.

My mom laughs, amused by my discomfort. "Anyway, how are you feeling about this semester? You know you're starting off with a 4.0."

I did pretty well in school, mostly A's and B's, and as a junior, this is my first semester with almost solely classes from my major, which I'm excited about. Psychology is such a fascinating subject to learn about.

"Yeah, I'm feeling pretty good about it," I reply, thankful for the change of topic.

"Just do your best, and everything else will fall into place," she says before sipping her orange juice. "You have to savor these days, they'll go by in a blink of an eye. Before you know it you'll be grown, married, and popping out my grandbabies."

"Oh, mom," I say, beyond exasperated, as she continues to laugh in amusement.

The next morning comes, and I make sure all my stuff is packed and ready to go. Usually I'd ride back with Tristan, but now I have my own car, so we're driving separately. The summer was nice. I accomplished everything I sought out to accomplish, but now I'm ready for the fall semester. "On to better things," I think to myself as I drive off to the next adventure.

THE WELCOME BACK PARTY

It's move-in day for the fall semester. Move-in day brings an unmistakable liveliness in the air. It's a fresh slate, a blank canvas, and I'm ready to take full advantage. Tristan and I are rooming together again, but I get to the building first. It's one of the recently built buildings on campus, so it's pretty nice. Thankfully, we're going to be living on the 5th floor, which is the top floor. There's nothing more annoying than being woken up in the middle of the night to the sounds of people having sex in the floor above you. Especially when you're not having any yourself.

Speaking of awkward sex situations, Tristan and I each have our own separate rooms within the unit. Our freshman year, we had to share a bedroom, which got awkward whenever he had a girl over. Usually I'd just have to wait in the common area for them to be done. I'm glad we won't have to do that anymore. Maybe I'll even have some girls of my own over this year.

I get into my room and look around. I always like move-in day, the moments before I start to unpack, when everything is still really clean, quiet, and new. No memories have been made yet, but you know you're going for a ride.

I've been unpacking for a few minutes when I hear Tristan come in. "Aye yo, Roman," he says excitedly. "You ready to be on demon time this year?" When Tristan heard about what happened with Jade, he had vowed to get me around as many women as possible so I could try to forget about her. "A guy I know is throwing a welcome back house party tonight, we definitely gotta go," Tristan says as he goes to put down his bags.

"I don't know, I feel like I need a warmup. I can't go right into a massive party from jump," I say as I continue to fold and put away my clothes.

"Do you think Jade needs a warm up? She's probably out on a date with one of your teammates right now, making fun of the way you shoot left handed layups."

"Are you—are you talking about Liz right now?" I ask. Liz, the girl that Tristan's still not over.

Tristan suddenly seems to be interested in our hallway carpeting. "Who, me? Liz? No way. What would make you ask such a thing?"

"Well, I don't have any teammates, I'm not playing sports right now."

"Oh yeah, right. I meant metaphorical teammates of course," Tristan says clearly rattled. "But that's besides the point. The point is, this is a perfect opportunity to meet new women. The best way to get over someone is to meet someone better. Everyone knows that," says Tristan self assuredly.

"I don't know, I think I might just see what Camryn's doing tonight. She's new here, I don't want her to be alone."

"That's perfect," says Tristan. "Tell her she can come to the party too. She's cute, it's about time you made your move."

"She still has a boyfriend. And besides, we're just friends," I say pointedly.

"She's really still doing the long distance thing? That'll never work," says Tristan. "But still, you should invite her. It'll be fun."

Tristan and I go to pick up Camryn from her dorm. I'm driving, which feels weird, but seeing as I don't drink, I'm the unofficial all time designated driver. Now that I have my own car, that's a title that I assume will stay with me for the foreseeable future. I have mixed feelings about that. For one, driving around with other people in the car always makes me nervous. Also, while talking to girls may be hard for me, driving and watching over drunk people is just as hard.

We get to Camryn's dorm, and she walks to the car. She's wearing a Lauryn Hill shirt, and jean shorts. Typical party attire. She gets in, and we set off for the house party as "Sicko Mode" plays in the background.

Cars line the roads as we get closer to the party. I feel butterflies in my stomach as I look for a place to park. I always feel anxious before stepping into a social event like this. Usually I just stand by the wall during parties. The alcohol, the loud music, the dancing, it's easy for me to feel overwhelmed. So my goal is to stay off to the side, out of the way.

We get to the door, and it's just as I imagined. Chaos. We're immediately greeted by a shirtless guy, who stumbles past us, and throws up in the nearest bushes. The music blares as we get inside. The bass is so deep that I can feel it in my bones. The smell of alcohol hangs heavily in the air. The lights are off, with the exception of white, string lights, like the ones you see at christmas, that are hanging on the walls. It would almost look cool, if not for the incredible amount of people inside.

We make our way through the swarm of people. It's so thickly packed that it feels like we're swimming in human bodies. We get to the kitchen area which is thankfully empty for the most part.

"Okay, Rome, I want you to leave tonight with at least 3 numbers. I know that doesn't seem like a lot, but I'm trying to start you off small," says Tristan. "Camryn, I know you got a man, but I'm trying to get Roman to stop thinking about you-know-who. So please assist in any way you can."

"Camryn, come on, tell Tristan he's being crazy. It's a madhouse in here," I say desperately.

Camryn shrugs. "I don't know Roman, you do need to get over Jade. The best way to get over someone is to find someone new."

"See, I told you!" Tristan says with a grin. "Everyone knows it." I've found that Tristan tends to get overly excited whenever alcohol gets in his system.

We make our way out to the sea of people, when we hear someone call out. "Aye, Tristan, what's up?" The voice is coming from one of Tristan's basketball teammates, Dalton. He walks over to us from the other side of the kitchen. He's wearing black joggers, a camouflage t-shirt, with a gold chain, and sunglasses on. Yes, sunglasses on while we're inside. Dalton, who prefers to go by DJ, is one of those white guys who tries to act black. He speaks with a blaccent, has a bald fade with a lighting bolt shaved into the side, and is infamously known for walking around campus blasting NBA Youngboy from his phone. He's the type of white guy who walks around with a durag on. I don't care for Dalton, but him and Tristan are pretty tight, unfortunately.

"Aye DJ, what's up?" Tristan asks, as he and Dalton dap each other up.

"Not much, just checking out the talent," he says while eyeing Camryn for an uncomfortably long time. "What's yo name shorty?" Dalton asks Camryn, the smarminess oozing out of him.

Camryn looks at Dalton with disdain. "Yeah, I think I'm going to go wait outside for a minute," she says before making her way out the side door.

"What's up with her?" I hear Dalton ask as I go to join her.

The side door in the kitchen leads out to a patio. There's a completely different energy once I get outside. The inside is packed to the gills, with loud music and a strong stench of alcohol. Outside, however, there are only a few people. There's a serenity in the air, as well as the smell of weed as the space is mostly occupied by smokers hanging out and talking. I spot Camryn standing off to the side, smoking by herself. She looks like something's bothering her.

"Are you good? Did Dalton get to you that much?" I ask as I walk up to her.

Camryn sighs. "No. Well, yes. Well, kind of. I don't know. Things aren't going well with Justin, and meeting that abomination in there reminded me of the type of people I'd have to deal with if Justin and I break up," Camryn says somberly while taking a hit from her joint.

"I'm sorry to hear that," I say sincerely. Throughout the summer we've mostly talked about my problems with women, namely Jade, while neglecting her issues she'd been having. I feel guilty. Normally I don't like to be around people when they're smoking, but I'm determined to be there for her like she was there for me all summer.

"Yeah, it's just weird. You know what I mean? We've been together for almost three years. We started dating in high school, but then he moved across the country to Wyoming, and we've been long distance ever since," she says, pausing to take another hit from her joint. "Long distance is hard, but after a while you kind of get used to it. We were long distance for two and a half years, but now it just feels like it's too much. Or I guess, it's not enough. Not enough time spent together, and too much work to sustain it."

"I can imagine how hard that'd be. I was kind of surprised that you didn't transfer somewhere close to him," I say.

"That's one of the reasons we're having problems. I wanted to transfer to a big school that's relatively close to my family. I didn't want to move across the country," says Camryn. "It's just been too hard to maintain. We barely get to see each other," she says with sadness written on her face. The kind of sadness that someone has when one of their grandparents dies of cancer. The situation is sad, but you've had time to come to terms with it. That's how Camryn sounds talking about her relationship with Justin.

"So you're going to end it?"

"Yeah, I mean what choice do I have? Soon I'll be out here forced to talk to guys like DJ," Camryn says, rolling her eyes.

"Not necessarily. All of us guys aren't as bad as Dalton."

"I guess you're right. I should probably stay single for a while anyway," she says while heading back inside. "Now let's go find some girls for you. I need the distraction."

We get inside and it's still as raucous as it was when we first got there. There's no one in the kitchen area, so God only knows what Tristan and Dalton got themselves into. We make our way through the crowd in the halls, past the area where people are playing beer pong, into the main area where people are dancing. That many people in a confined space, constantly moving around, caused the air in the room to become very humid. I already feel myself sweating.

"Come on, Roman, you have to dance," Camryn says while trying to pull me into the middle of the room. "You're not going to meet anyone pressed up against the wall like that."

I shrug. "I'm not going to meet anyone by dancing either. I have no rhythm, plus I'm already sweating. It's hot as hell in here."

Camryn goes off on her own to meet people, and I spend time being a wallflower, like I'm used to. My mind wanders to what Camryn told me earlier in the night. She's going to be single soon, and going to the same school I go to. What does that mean for our relationship? I've never been able to stay friends with a girl that's single before, especially a girl that I'm somewhat attracted to like Camryn. Can our friendship survive? It was easier when she had a boyfriend, because I didn't have to think about this sort of thing. I look over to see her talking to a pretty red-haired girl, gesturing towards me. Maybe having a girl who's a friend has its advantages.

While I'm standing there watching Camryn with the red-haired girl, I see a flash of blue coming from one of the windows. "Cops!" I hear someone yell. That's when all hell breaks loose. A mass of bodies surges towards the back doors all at once, blocking the clear view I had of Camryn a second ago. I do my best not to get stampeded as I look around for Tristan and Camryn. One of the main responsibilities of being the DD is being the getaway driver if the cops come.

I stumble outside frantically looking around as I feel a massive wave of people stream by me to safety. I see Tristan pretty quickly. The height of basketball players makes them easy to find in situations like this. Unfortunately, I see he still has Dalton with him as he makes his way over to me. Soon after, Camryn bumps into me holding up a scrap of paper. "I got a number for you," she says as we scramble away. As we get closer to the car, I realize that we didn't even need to run away like that considering Camryn and Tristan are both twenty-one, and while I'm not yet twenty-one, I'm sober. Still, if everyone is running, it's probably a good idea to run too.

We make it to the car and I'm displeased to find that Dalton is still with Tristan, but there's no time to stop so we all just load up the car. Nobody says anything until we make it out of the neighborhood. Almost as if we all felt like us being quiet in the car would help us escape. It sounds silly, but maybe it did help, because we made it out of the neighborhood without a hitch.

"So what's the move?" asks Dalton from the back seat.

"I'm thinking we go home," I say. It's a little after 1 in the morning now, which isn't super late, but I'm ready to get in bed.

"Ahh come on, man. Let's hit up Cookout at least," says Tristan. Cookout is the go to late night spot for college kids after a party.

"Camryn how are you feeling?" I ask, hoping she says she wants to go back to her dorm too.

"Actually Cookout sounds nice. Maybe the girl I met at the party will be there. I can introduce you," Camryn says with excitement.

We pull into Cookout, and the parking lot is pretty packed. 1:00 - 3:00 AM is prime Cookout hours. We wait in line, and I get a peanut butter fudge milkshake which isn't the healthiest option considering it's technically the middle of the night, but I figure I burned enough calories by running from the cops to make it somewhat passable. We sit down at a round table silently reliving the night's events while we enjoy our various Cookout items.

"Oh yeah, Roman, check out this number I got for you. It's from the girl with the red hair I was talking to. She thought you were cute," says Camryn as she hands me the slip of paper that she was trying to show me as we were making our escape. I take the paper Camryn hands me, with anticipation. The girl she was talking to was really pretty, she kind of looked like Isla Fisher's character from the *Wedding Crashers* movie. As I look down at the paper I see that somehow the paper had gotten wet, and smudged half the numbers.

I sigh. "I can't read all the numbers."

"I'm so sorry, it was so dark, I didn't even realize," says Camryn. Her voice tinged with disappointment. "I couldn't even get her name, I was in too much of a rush because of the cops."

"Since you lost her number, how about I give you my number instead," says Dalton while winking at Camryn.

"I think I'm good, actually," says Camryn with contempt.

"Speaking of women, guess who I ran into at the party," Tristan says while taking a bite of his burger. "Liv."

"Who's Liv?" asks Camryn.

"Oh, she's the girl Tristan's in love with," I say with a grin.

"Yeah yeah, very funny," says Tristan sarcastically.

"Alright, so how did it go?" I ask.

"Well, she wants to start hanging again soon, so we'll see how it goes." Tristan says it nonchalantly, but I can see the spark in his eyes that's been missing for a while.

"Aye, she's a fine piece of ass. That's what's up," says Dalton.

I roll my eyes at Dalton's comment. "Yeah I'm happy for you, for real."

The rest of the night goes by smoothly. I drop off Dalton and Camryn at their dorms, and then Tristan and I make our way back to ours. We wearily trudge our way to our room, which is at the end of the hall.

"So you had fun tonight?" Tristan asks groggily.

"Yeah, it wasn't too bad," I say with a shrug.

"I know you don't like DJ, but he's my teammate so I gotta be nice," says Tristan.

"Yeah, I understand. Still a good way to start the semester," I say as we get to the door to our dorm.

"You'll be completely over Jade in no time," he says. Giving a slight wave before going into his room.

"I sure hope he's right," I think to myself as I go into mine.

THE FIRST DAY OF CLASS

It's the first day of class, and I'm walking to class with Tristan. It's a nice day out, and the campus is full of energy as people are excitedly making their way to their first class of the semester. My schedule's looking pretty good for the semester. I have two classes on Monday/Wednesday/Friday, and three classes on Tuesday/Thursday. Thankfully I have no super early or late classes. My earliest class is at 9:30 today.

I also have an internship that I'm starting today. I'm going to be working at an off campus counseling center. I know it's just an internship, but it'll be my first time working in psychology, which I'm happy about. I may have confidence issues in certain aspects of my life, but I am confident that psychology is the right major for me.

"I'm so tired man, these early morning workouts always kill me," says Tristan. As a student athlete, he has a strenuous schedule. Workouts at 6:00 AM, and practice at 4:00 PM every day with meetings in between.

"It'll be worth it once the season starts and you're blowing everybody out," I say with a shrug.

"It better be. Year three of this, I need it to start paying off."

"Yeah I understand. We still meeting for dinner at the dining hall after your practice?"

"I'll let you know. It depends on how tired I am," says Tristan as we approach the building where my first class is. "Oh, and Roman, make sure you keep your eyes open. It's a new semester, lots of single women walking around," he says as I go to walk into the building.

I'm in my second class of the day, social psych. I'm trying to pay attention because the first thing the professor says is that she refuses to use any sort of visual aids during her lectures. So all of the notes are coming from her verbally. It seems like it'll make the class unnecessarily difficult, but it's the class I'm most looking forward to this semester. I have to go directly from my first class of the day, Brain and Behavior, to this class. It's within the same building so it's not a far walk, but as someone that likes to get to class a minimum of fifteen minutes early, I can tell it's going to get old fast. There's nothing worse than being one of the last people in class and having to sit in the front row. How can I slack off on my phone now? The teacher is for sure going to catch me and call me out.

The professor starts going over the syllabus and I try to find a way to get comfortable. The seats are really close together, but luckily the seat to my left is empty. I'm right in the middle though, so I can't help but make awkward eye contact with the professor as she's talking. The professor starts going over our weekly quiz assignments when the door opens. There's only a couple seats left now, the one next to me, and one back in the 4th row. I desperately don't want to be sandwiched between two people so I'm hoping whoever this person is chooses the seat in the 4th row. That is, until I see who it is.

The student walks in and I see it's a girl, who looks to be around my age. She has olive skin, honey brown eyes, and curly dark hair. Her high cheekbones give her an elegant air. She's beautiful in a way that you don't see everyday, in a way that even most celebrities aren't. She embodies beauty. Her aura, her very existence is beauty. I realize that it's the same girl I tried to talk to on the last day before summer break.

She looks around the class for a seat. For most other people, being late means they show up looking disheveled, or at least a little out of sorts, but this girl is different. She carries herself gracefully, like royalty, and she casually saunters in my direction. Upon her entrance into the class, I momentarily forgot that there's an open seat next to me and once I realize that, I feel myself start to panic. My face burns with embarrassment as I remember the day a few months ago when I inexplicably told this girl who I'd never met before to have a good summer. Hopefully she doesn't remember, or at least I hope she isn't able to recognize me. Although now that I think about it, I guess it's worse to just be forgotten. To be viewed as just another strange guy that she's come across in her life.

My nerves are unbearable, my heart feels like it's about to jump out of my chest. I try to remind myself to breathe as she gets to the seat next to me and sits down. I can feel the pressure of her presence next to me. I can smell her vanilla and cinnamon scented perfume. The seats are so close together that our arms are almost touching. I try to focus on what the professor's saying, like I should be doing anyway, but I can't. The words just go in one ear, and out the other. I'm too busy thinking about how I should handle this situation. Of all the people that go to the school, what are the odds that she would be the one sitting next to me? This mystery girl who's haunted me since that day in the quad. Maybe this is my second chance.

There's only a few more minutes of class left, and the professor is wrapping things up. I've been going over how I'm going to approach the mystery girl, rehearsing what I'm gonna say in my head over and over again. *Hey, my name is Roman, I just wanted to say you're really pretty, and wanted to know if you would like to go on a date sometime.* Short, simple, and to the point. It's easy, just a simple sentence. But should I acknowledge that afternoon a few months ago in the quad? Should I just ignore it and hope she forgot about it? Maybe if I bring it up, she'll think I'm some stalker who somehow found out she was taking this class and decided to take it too, as a way to get close to her. No, that doesn't make sense, this isn't some spy movie. Man, there's no way I can try to talk to her in this state of mind, maybe I can just try to get her name so I can stop thinking about her as "Mystery Girl" in my head.

The professor dismisses the class, and I prepare myself to make my move. "Hey, my name is Roman. What's your name?" I recite to myself as I go to pick up my bag. I turned to where she was sitting for the big moment, only to find that the seat was empty. I look up just in time to see her walk out of the class. Another missed opportunity.

It's an hour later. I got back to my dorm just in time to get ready for my internship. It's my first day and I'm feeling kind of nervous. Over the summer, I looked for jobs I could work during the school year. Last year I worked as a dishwasher, and while it ultimately helped me save enough to get a car, I kind of hated it, sure it had its perks, like free food, but college women aren't impressed by a man who works as a dishwasher. Plus, I wanted something that was related to my major. So it was time to move on. I found this counseling center through research and pure luck. By research, I mean I basically just googled "psychology places near me," set my location as my school, and sent an email to all the places I could find. Of course I tried the more traditional method of applying through Indeed, but after the fifth rejection email, I decided to take things into my own hands. Thankfully, one of the places I emailed got back to me, and we were able to set this position up. It's 15 minutes away from campus, and if I didn't have a car there's no way I could have gotten this position. So in a way I guess I should be thankful for the dishwashing job.

I don't have many passable professional clothing items, so I walk into the office for my first day as an intern, wearing a super baggy long sleeve, white button up shirt that belonged to my dad, and black slacks, that make me feel like I'm melting in the 90 degree August heat. I can feel myself sweating as I get inside, but after working so hard to get the job, I don't want to mess things up.

After a few minutes of sitting in the waiting area, a middle aged woman, wearing a light blue blouse with plaid pants walks out.

"Hi, you must be Roman. I'm Dr. Phillips," she says while extending her hand.

"Nice to meet you," I say while shaking her hand.

After the introduction, she takes me on a tour of the office. It's a relatively small counseling center, they only have three therapists working there. Dr. Phillips explains that I'll be sort of like a secretary for the office. Answering calls, setting appointments, helping to sort files, and handling general things that the therapists need, like picking up lunch orders. My hours are going to be 12-4, Monday through Friday. Overall it seems like a chill place to work. My first day is kind of like a practice run through of what my normal tasks are going to be, so Dr. Phillips lets me go after an hour.

It's now half past two, and I'm walking to the gym. The campus is busiest during early to mid afternoon. Full of students heading to class, or the dining hall, or wherever. I missed this aspect of college. It's full of life, and feeling that energy makes me feel revitalized. I can tell this semester is going to be a lot of work. I'll have class, then the internship, then the gym, and then home-work assignments due throughout the week, every week.

I'll also have my comic club meetings every thursday. Which is basically a club for dorks like myself who like comics. We meet up to discuss different comic book movies, and shows, as well as some ongoing anime. We also work on our own manga panels and comic strips. The guys I've met in the club have helped me with the comic I'm submitting in the contest. Especially these two guys Wayne and Dante, who are probably the closest I've come to making friends on campus.

I'm kind of looking forward to all the work I'll have to do though. Whenever I'm busy and productive, it gives me less time to make questionable decisions in other aspects of my life, like in my love life. Maybe things would've worked out better with Jade if I had more things to occupy my mind over the summer. Now that I'll be so busy, maybe I won't even feel the urge to go after anyone romantically. It'll be nice not having to feel rejection for a while.

I get to the gym, and unlike the rest of the campus, there's not a lot of people inside. The early afternoon is right before the time it gets really busy. It feels good to have a release. I'm not sure what I'd do without the gym. I'm standing at the squat rack, getting ready for my next set, when I catch a glimpse of some-one with flaming red hair walking down the stairs into the weight lifting area. It's the girl I saw Camryn talking to at the party the other day.

She's even prettier than I remember. She must think I'm an asshole for never texting her, although it's possible she just doesn't remember giving out her number at all. I know things can be cloudy for people when they've been drinking. I consider going over to talk to her. After all she had thought I was cute enough to give out her number, but I can't seem to bring myself to do it. The party was pretty dark, and she probably was drinking, so she probably didn't even really see me. Yeah that makes sense, imagine, a girl like that thinking I'm cute enough to want to talk to? That's just laughable. If I go over there now, I'd probably just embarrass myself. I should probably be avoiding women right now anyway. I don't think I can handle a rejection like that so soon after Jade.

I go through the rest of my workout without a hitch. Quickly wiping the red haired girl from my thoughts. There's no sense in fantasizing about a girl I have no chance with. After my workout, I go to my locker to get my things to leave, when I hear a voice from behind me.

"Hey, you're the guy from the party right?" It's the red haired girl I saw walking into the gym earlier.

"Yeah, what's up? I'm Roman," I say, trying to sound as cool as possible while masking my surprise. Up close I can see she has really nice green eyes. Like the leaves of a tree in the middle of spring, when they've just grown back. She has little freckles on her nose and cheeks that I find to be cute.

"Hey, I'm Olivia," she says with a smile. "So you just like to get people's numbers and never text them?"

"Yeah, sorry about that. When my friend gave it to me, half of the numbers had gotten smudged."

"Well, how about I give it to you again? I can put it directly into your phone this time."

I hand her phone, and watch as she types in the numbers. "Okay, I'm going to call you just to make sure it's the right one," I say, partially thinking this is some kind of prank someone is pulling on me.

Her phone rings, showing it's the real number. "Cool, now I expect you to text me tonight," she says while giving me a playful shove.

I walk back to my dorm in shock over what just happened. It's hard for me to imagine a girl like Olivia would be interested enough in me to go out of her way to talk to me. I'd have to be an idiot not to text her. So much for avoiding women, I think to myself with a smile.

THE SHOPPING SPREE

It's Friday, the end of the first week of class. Even though we're roommates, this is my first time seeing Tristan all week, because of both of our schedules. Camryn, Tristan, and I are at the dining hall getting dinner together, talking about what happened to us this week. Dalton's there too, but I'm trying to pretend like he's not.

"How do you like your roommate?" I ask Camryn, as I take a bite out of my grilled chicken.

"She's a little weird, not gonna lie. We're not supposed to have pets in the dorms, but she snuck in her pet lizard. There's also been this strange smell coming from her room, but I mean, she leaves me alone for the most part so I guess I can't complain too much," she says with a shrug. "I think I'm going to join the Black Student Union to meet some people."

"Whatchu trying to meet people for? I'm the only guy you need to meet," says Dalton with a smirk.

Camryn gives him a dirty look. "Just eat your food, dude."

"Man, I'm so tired. I'm glad it's the weekend so I can have a break from classes," says Tristan.

"It's only been a week, you're already this tired?" I ask, while working on my spinach.

"The first week is always the hardest, I just have to push through."

"It's not the workouts that have him worn out, he's been linking up with Liz," says Dalton.

"DJ, chill out, I'm trying to be lowkey about it," says Tristan. He says it jokingly, but in the way he does when he's in an uncomfortable situation, and is trying to deflect. It could just be my imagination, but it looked as if he glanced at Camryn as he said it. I make a mental note to ask him about it later.

"So how do you feel about her? Do you think it's like the real thing?" I ask. It's funny to me how just a few months ago we had a similar conversation about Jade, except he was the one asking these questions.

"I don't know, I'm trying not to get my hopes up, but it feels different than the first time we got together," Tristan says while taking a bite out of his grilled cheese.

"My little Tristan's all grown up," I say jokingly.

"Yeah yeah yeah, but enough about me. Have you met any new girls since the semester started?"

"I ran into the girl from the party at the gym, and she gave me her number. Her name is Olivia," I say while feeling the blood rush to my face. For some reason I always feel super awkward whenever I talk about things happening in my life, especially things related to women.

"I have a class with her," says Dalton. "She's fine as hell, you better lock that down before someone else does."

Camryn rolls her eyes at Dalton's comment. "How have things been going with her?"

"We've been texting pretty consistently, and have a date set up for Sunday."

"Perfect, so we still have a day to prepare. We should go to the mall tomorrow to practice. I'll help you get your outfit together," says Camryn.

"Okay mom," I say jokingly. I can tell I won't be able to change her mind on this.

It's after dinner, and Tristan and I are walking back to our dorm.

"Do you have to bring Dalton with you everywhere you go now? I know team chemistry is important, but he's a little annoying," I say.

Tristan laughs. "Roman, you think everyone's annoying. In high school, people would always ask me why you didn't talk to them. If you gave DJ a chance you'd see he's not so bad."

Tristan bringing up high school brings back a rush of memories that I had been repressing. It feels like so long ago, almost like a past life. Sitting alone at lunch while Tristan was off being summoned by all of his other friends, which was a significant number. Everyone wanted to be friends with Tristan, it was different for me though. I recall all the hurtful nicknames and jokes. Never feeling like I fit in with my teammates or classmates. Sasha, my long term crush who I had asked to prom over text, only to get rejected and have her send out the screenshot of it to all of her friends, which then ended up being seen by half the school after it got posted on Twitter. Maybe that's why I feel so much disdain for Dalton. He reminds me of so many people from my high school. The only useful thing I got out of high school was learning the importance of self protection. Which is why I value my friendship with Tristan and Camryn so much. It's rare that I feel so comfortable around other people.

"Ugh, don't remind me of highschool. What a nightmare that was. Speaking of one of our mutual friends, did something happen between you and Camryn?" I ask, suddenly remembering the question I meant to ask him at dinner.

For a second, Tristan wears an expression that looks almost like guilt, but it quickly passes. "Oh, nothing, just feels kind of weird talking about women in front of other women you know?"

While me and Camryn have talked extensively about a lot of things, including women in my love life, it's kind of a new phenomenon for Tristan who has spent most of his life only being around girls in a romantic context. So it makes sense for him to say something like that, but at the same time, it feels like he's holding something back. I decide not to press him about it any further. At least not right now. "So you and Liz huh? Does this feel more fulfilling than running through all those girls did?" I ask.

"Yeah, I don't know, I guess. I feel like maybe if things progress further, then I'll start to feel differently," says Tristan. "It was a nice ride, but I feel like I need to get off the streets soon. How about you and Olivia though? How does she compare to Jade?"

"She seems cool, but I don't know, I need to see what our date is like first I think," I say with a shrug. It's crazy to me how much I've grown since the beginning of the summer. If this situation with Olivia had happened back in the winter, or even the spring before I went home for the summer, I would probably already be infatuated. "Do you remember the girl I told you about a couple months ago? From the beginning of summer?" I ask Tristan.

"The one from the quad who had you stumbling over your words? Yeah, what about her?"

"I have a class with her, I sat next to her on the first day actually."

"Oh really? That's what's up," says Tristan excitedly. "Look at you, two new girls in one week, I'm proud. So you got her number?"

I look down at my shoes. "Not exactly."

"Her Instagram? Her Snapchat?"

"No to both of those things," I say dejectedly.

Tristan sighs. "Did you at least get her name?"

"No, see, it all happened too fast. By the time class ended and I tried to talk to her, she was gone."

"Come on, Rome. I taught you better than that," says Tristan with disappointment in his voice. "Well at least you got that Olivia girl's number. I still think you should try to talk to that mystery girl too though."

"We'll see, I don't have as much game as you though so I don't know how that'll work out," I say as we walk up to our room.

"You just have to believe in yourself. The girl's already like you, you just have to capitalize, for real," says Tristan, stopping to look at me outside our door. "You know that character from *Sky High* who gets labeled a sidekick because she's afraid to use her powers, even though she's like, the strongest character? Well that's you. You just have to not be afraid to use your powers."

What powers could I possibly have, except the power to make girls not like me? It's the morning after our group dinner at the dining hall, and I'm getting ready to go to the mall with Camryn, but I can't stop thinking about what Tristan said to me last night. Okay, maybe I'm a little cautious when it comes to approaching girls, but isn't that the smart way to be? You can't just charge head first into situations that you think will lead to pain. Caution is what keeps people from touching hot stoves, and stepping into oncoming traffic. It's what keeps me from almost certain disaster whenever I see a pretty girl. I think back to that day in the quad when I approached the mystery girl. If I had exercised the right amount of caution, I could've saved myself a lot of embarrassment.

But another part of me thinks that maybe Tristan is right. Maybe the only thing separating guys like Tristan from guys like me isn't that they're better than me, or more charismatic, but the fact that they're able to overcome the fear that I feel. It's a lot easier to assume that women don't like me than to actually try to talk to them. Sometimes I just feel like I'm unlovable. I feel that once they get somewhat close, and get to know me, they'll run in the opposite direction. Like Jade did.

"How are things with you and your boyfriend now?" I ask Camryn. We're at the mall now, checking out the clothes at H&M.

Camryn sighs. "At this point it seems like it's over, and we're both just too scared to admit it."

"So Dalton will finally have a shot with you soon?" I ask jokingly.

Camryn gives me a dirty look, not finding my joke amusing. "I just don't understand why he's always hanging around Tristan."

"I really don't like him, but Tristan looks at it like a team bonding thing," I say while looking at some of the graphic t-shirts.

"I hate how he always tries to hit on me even though I don't show the slightest interest. How do guys have so much confidence?" asks Camryn.

"Don't ask me, I asked this girl to prom and she laughed in my face and said that the thought of going to prom with me made her uncomfortable. That was enough to make me not want to ask anyone out for a while."

"I'm trying to find the silver lining, but that's a pretty terrible story," says Camryn while looking through the chino pants. "Maybe if Dalton keeps hanging out with us, some of his confidence will rub off on you. What do you think of these?" she asks while holding up a pair of navy blue chinos.

"I don't know, they're not really my style," I say with a shrug.

Camryn rolls her eyes. "Yeah, I know that, so far all I've seen you wear are shorts and joggers."

"To be fair you've mostly only seen me at work, and it's been hot."

"Yeah but still. Don't you remember the practice date we went on? You were wearing shorts and a tank top."

"In my defense, I didn't know I was supposed to dress like it was an actual date," I say with a slight laugh.

"That was the whole point," says Camryn with exasperation. "Anyway, we need to up your wardrobe if you want to impress Olivia. Yeah, I think you're a large. What do you think of this shirt?" she asks while holding up a light blue, long sleeve dress shirt.

"What am I going on an interview?" I ask with a slight grin.

Camryn rolls her eyes again. "Just try it on and let me see."

I put on the shirt, and come out of the dressing room. It felt nice wearing a dress shirt that wasn't two sizes too big, like the one I wore the other day to my internship. "Hmm, I like the fit, but I think you need a different color," says Camryn. "Try these," she says, holding up a black polo style shirt, and a navy blue turtleneck.

I try them on, and come out of the dressing room. "Yeah, those look good on you," says Camryn. "How do you like them?"

I shrug. "I'm not that picky when it comes to clothes. Anything that women will think I look good in is good enough for me," I say on my way to the checkout line. I end up getting the shirts Camryn picked out along with a couple other shirts, and a few pairs of the chino pants.

"How are you with shoes? Do you need more, or do you have some nice pairs already?" asks Camryn while looking down at my old Nike Blazers. "Yeah, I think we need to look at shoes."

We walk into the DSW, and Camryn ignores all of the sneakers and goes right for the more formal shoes. "Sneakers are good for activity dates like laser tag, bowling, or picnics, but for a dinner or brunch date you need something more formal," she says while picking up a pair of Chelsea boots. "What do you think of these?"

"No Chelsea boots. I don't mind boots generally, but they have to have laces or they look weird to me."

"Okay, that's understandable. Just keep in mind that, we're going for a clean cut, simple look for you. If you have the wrong shoes, the whole outfit falls apart," says Camryn while examining a pair of Doc Martens.

"I kind of like these," I say while holding up a pair of low cut, brown leather shoes that say they were made by Steve Madden.

"Hmm, yeah those could work. Try them on."

I find the shoes in my size and try them on. They're not as comfortable as my Nikes, but they look pretty nice, so I decide to get them.

"Please no more shopping today, I'm tired, and if I spend any more money, I won't even be able to go on the date," I say as we leave DSW.

"Okay, okay, we can be done now. I think she'll be impressed. Just remember, on this date, you have to be yourself. That's the most important thing."

"I don't know it didn't work out too well with Jade," I reply glumly.

"You have to forget about Jade, she wasn't good enough for you anyway."

"Tristan says I have hidden superpowers, maybe I should use those on the date with Olivia," I say with a shrug.

"Yeah well, maybe Tristan's right. You can't let yourself over-think about girls you're into," says Camryn pointedly. "All it does is feed into your insecurities, and block yourself from your potential, or your super powers, as you call them ."

"I don't know. I guess I'm just afraid that even my "true potential" won't be enough, and the girls I like still won't like me back, and choose guys like Tristan over me."

Camryn laughs, catching me off guard. "You have to stop being so melodramatic. Sure, Tristan is a cool guy, he's charismatic, and charming. But if you would just stop getting in your own way, you would see that you're those things too, just in a different way."

"Maybe you're right. I mean, the fact that a girl like Olivia practically demanded that I get her number, and ask her out, has to count for something."

"Exactly, and besides, we wouldn't be friends if I didn't think you were a cool and interesting guy to be around," Camryn says with a shrug.

I get back to my dorm feeling significantly more optimistic about my date with Olivia after the talks I had with Tristan and Camryn. I have a car, I have new clothes that I look good in. I feel Jade slowly slipping from my mind as I embrace this evolved version of myself. I think I'm ready to stop getting in my own way.

THE INVITATION

It's the morning of my date with Olivia. We're going for brunch, which is a new experience for me. I've only had a couple of dates in my life and they've all been at night, or at least late afternoon. I'm feeling kind of nervous, but this nervousness feels different than the nervous I felt before my first date with Jade. With Jade, I felt like I was out of my depth, like I was doing something completely foreign that I wasn't prepared for, and any minor slip up would ruin the whole date. Plus there was the whole thing with the rain, and having to change plans at the last minute. This time I just feel more comfortable and at ease, but still excited.

I look into my closet to pick out what to wear. Normally I'd just wear a t-shirt and jeans, but after my trip to the mall with Camryn, my whole wardrobe has been upgraded. I pick out a navy blue polo shirt, and light gray chinos with a plaid pattern. Hopefully Camryn's right, and Olivia likes the clothes I pick out.

I'm in the car going to pick up Olivia. In psychology class we talked about how it's possible for people to zone out while they're driving, not remembering how they ended up at their destination. That's how I feel as I wait outside for Olivia. She lives in one of the student apartments that are within walking distance of campus.

I see her walk out towards my car. The sun refracts beautifully off of her long, flowing, red hair, making it look as if it's glowing like an inferno, or a sunset on a summer day. She's wearing a green floral romper that perfectly compliments her emerald eyes, and light brown wedges. Her tan makes her ivory skin look almost golden.

She gets to the car and I feel the usual butterflies that usually accompany me whenever I go on a date. She opens the door to get in.

"Hey," she says with a smile.

"Hey, you look really pretty."

"Thank you. You smell really good. What cologne do you wear?"

"Oh, you know, just deodorant and soap." I actually have on this Tom Ford cologne that my mom got me for my last birthday, but for some reason I want Olivia to think I just smell like this all the time.

"Have you heard Travis Scott's new album, *Astroworld*?" I ask as The Weeknd sings the hook to the song "Wake up" in the background. "He's one of my favorite artists, I felt like I was having an out of body experience the first time I listened to it."

I feel like someone's music taste says a lot about them, and having similar music tastes with someone you're trying to date is a good sign. Plus it gives us something to talk about.

"He's okay, I've still only heard that one song he did with Drake."

"What artists do you like?"

"I really like Ariana Grande, her new album, *Sweetener*, just dropped and I'm super into it. I also like Mac Miller a lot, I've had his album *Swimming*, on repeat, which is probably why I haven't heard a lot of the Travis Scott album yet," she says with a shrug.

"That's interesting, I haven't heard the Ariana Grande album yet, but I'll have to check it out," I say. I barely know this girl, and she's already got me to commit to listening to a full Ariana Grande album. The things we do for love.

I drive into the parking lot of the restaurant, and it's pretty packed. Thankfully, Camryn advised me to make reservations beforehand while we were at the mall yesterday, so I'm hoping we won't have too long of a wait. Before we go to walk in, Olivia looks at me, and I realize this is the first time she's really gotten to see the clothes I picked out because it's kind of hard to see them while sitting in the car.

"You look nice. I'm impressed, most guys would just come in shorts and a t-shirt," Olivia says with another smile. Her words fill me with confidence. I'm again thankful for the help that Camryn gave me.

We get inside, and the restaurant is nice. There's a ton of windows and natural lighting. It feels like a very open space. There's a patio off to the side for people that want to eat outside, but I'm hoping Olivia wants to eat inside. I have a tendency of breaking into a nervous sweat on dates sometimes, and it's a warm day, so I didn't want to increase the chance of that happening.

"Hey, I have a reservation for two under the name Richardson," I say to the hostess.

I briefly recall how it was for my first date with Jade, I felt like a fish out of water, completely out of my element. That day, when I had to ask the hostess for a table, my voice came out so softly, I was shocked she could even hear me. Looking back, it reminds me of how I felt as a kid whenever I had to give a presentation in front of the class in school.

Today it feels different though, like radically different. Maybe it's because I'm here with Olivia instead of Jade, I think to myself as we walk to our table. With Jade I felt like I was playing some kind of guessing game, I was so unsure of myself during the whole time we were semi-dating. Olivia's been more open, maybe that's why I feel more comfortable in this situation. But I don't know, I feel like I've grown a lot over the last couple of months in my own right, it feels like it's more than the difference between Jade and Olivia. As we walk to our seats, similar to the dates I had with Jade, I feel people's eyes follow us. It still feels good, but unlike those times, where I felt out of place, like a bench player that suddenly had gotten subbed into the game, this time I feel at home, like I'm right where I'm meant to be. Where I deserve to be.

We get to our seats. I'm feeling generally more confident and comfortable with the whole dating experience, but there's still no preparing yourself for the feeling you get when you're sitting across from someone on a date. You can feel their eyes curiously studying you. Your facial features, your mannerisms, everything. It makes me feel naked and vulnerable, like I need to put on an extra layer of clothing. We order drinks first. I get water, and Olivia orders a mimosa. "Just water? You don't want juice, or something a little stronger?" asks Olivia, curiously.

"I don't drink, actually," I say. "Plus the water is good for my skin, it helps me maintain my youthful glow.".

"That's interesting, why don't you drink?"

"All of those D.A.R.E seminars really got to me," I say sarcastically. "Nah, but really I guess I just feel like I have an addictive personality. It's hard for me to do things in moderation and I don't feel confident in my ability to handle it." I think back to my past relationships with women. How out of control I felt. I felt like I had to text them or be around them constantly, to the point where I felt like I was smothering them. I think about how anxious I feel whenever I'm forced to take an unplanned day off from the gym. I definitely can see myself feeling similarly about drugs and alcohol if I let myself partake in that, but my lack of self control isn't the real reason, or at least not the main reason.

When I was growing up, I had an older cousin named Damian who I always looked up to, he was like an older brother to me. He's the one that first introduced me to superheroes. One night, when I was nine, we were coming home from the premiere showing of the new Spider-Man movie. Damian used to always take me to see the new superhero movies. It was late, and raining. On our way back home, we were blindsided by a drunk driver who ran a red light. Damian died in the accident. From that moment on, I vowed to never drink. I usually don't tell people that story because it understandably freaks them out. I hate to see the look of pity on their faces.

"Okay, yeah that makes sense," says Olivia.

"Yeah, most people think I have some dramatic reason for not doing it, but really it just comes down to me being a control freak who likes to have something that makes me feel different than other people," I say with a shrug. I know this explanation is only a half truth, but it'll have to do. At least for now.

"So does it bother you being around people who are drinking?" Olivia asks, while eyeing her mimosa hesitantly.

"I don't really care as long as no one tries to force me to drink."

"Oof, you would've hated my ex then. He was very domineering, always pressuring his friends to drink more than they wanted to."

This comment is interesting to me. Jade never brought up any of her ex's, but I guess that could just be because she mostly had shorter term relationships.

"Yeah, I don't think we would've gotten along," I say with a shrug. "How long were you guys together?"

"Two years. Up until this past March, but we were kind of shaky for a few months before that," she says while taking a sip of her mimosa.

"I'm sorry that happened–or well I guess I'm not sorry it happened because then we wouldn't have met, but I'm sorry you had to go through that," I say, slightly flustered.

Olivia laughs. "Yeah breakups suck, but it's cool, I'm over it. What about you though? Any bad exes?"

"I don't have any exes actually," I say, shamefully.

In my mind my lack of experience is a red flag. I couldn't find even one girl who wanted to be in a serious relationship with me? How pathetic. Plus there's the fact that I'm twenty, going on twenty-one, and still a virgin. What girl would want to be with a guy that has never had sex?

"That's interesting, why do you think you haven't had a serious relationship?" Olivia asks.

"Just bad luck I guess," I say as our food arrives. "Saved by the bell," I think to myself as the waiter places our food down on the table. I'm thankful to not have to answer her question in more detail. Women like guys who are faithful and won't go after other women, but I can't imagine that they'd like to hear that their date is a loser that can't get other women.

Our food looks good. I ordered a veggie omelet with a biscuit and fruit, and Olivia ordered a caesar salad. Anytime I'm lucky enough to eat out for breakfast, or in this case brunch, I make sure to get an omelet. Not just because they're typically healthy, but because I like them and don't know how to make them myself, so it's pretty much the only time I'm able to get it.

"A salad for brunch? I respect someone that eats healthy," I say while taking a bite out of my omelet.

"Yeah, I used to compete in beauty pageants, and eating healthy just became a habit over the years."

"A real life beauty queen, I knew there was something special about you."

Olivia's cheeks redden and she gives a soft chuckle. "Stop it," she says playfully, clearly pleased with my compliment. "Actually, this is a little embarrassing. I don't know if you noticed but I have a Hannah Montana sticker on my purse," she says holding up her purse and showing me the sticker. "When I was little and competing in pageants, I would pretend like I was Hannah Montana performing at a concert. Now the sticker is like my good luck charm."

"Are you one of those Disney adults who has an unhealthy attachment to all things Disney related?"

"I wouldn't say all that, but I'd be down for like a Disney movie marathon or something," Olivia says while taking a bite of her salad.

"Are you proposing a second date already?" I ask.

"Don't get ahead of yourself, I'm totally planning on ghosting you after this date," says Olivia jokingly.

"You're really going to ghost me after telling me your deep, dark, Hannah Montana secret?" I ask light-heartedly.

"We'll see," says Olivia as she laughs softly. "But Roman, I told you a secret of mine, now you owe me one of yours."

"Oh would you look at the time, it looks like it's time for me to go," I say.

"Ahh come on, don't be like that."

"Okay, okay, you're lucky I have a thing for cute redheads. Do you remember earlier when I said I didn't have on anything except for soap and deodorant? I actually have on cologne too."

"Oh, how terrible, I definitely have to ghost you now," Olivia says.

"So, I have an actual question for you," I say while taking a pause to sip my water. "Why did you decide to have Camryn give me your number at the party?"

"Well your friend Camryn really talked you up. She talked about how interesting and funny you were. And she said you were a stand up guy. Plus you were cute, and I kind of have a thing for tall, semi-awkward, cute guys, so I thought it was worth a shot.

It's not every day you have a girl talk up a guy so vehemently," says Olivia with a shrug. "If it was a guy that was trying to get my number for you, I probably would've said no."

I make a mental note to give Camryn a big hug next time I see her.

"So, now it's my turn for a question. What kind of relationship are you looking for?" Olivia asks.

It's the first time anyone's asked me that question before, and I never realized how hard it was to answer. It should be obvious, after all I've been telling myself I've been looking for a relationship forever, and I'm starting to really like Olivia. She's beautiful, she's cool, she's funny, but I feel like there's something holding me back from saying I want a relationship. Maybe it's just me being afraid that saying it so plainly will scare her off, or maybe it's something else. I don't know for sure.

"Honestly, I'm not really sure. I'm not opposed to a serious relationship, but I don't want to force anything," I say while taking a bite of my biscuit.

"Yeah, I think we're on the same page," Olivia says. "I feel like that's what everyone says though, when it's still early on, and you're afraid of what the other person will think. It's the safe answer."

"I agree, but I mean what am I supposed to do? Tell you that I'm in love with you and want to marry you on the first date?"

Olivia laughs. "I mean if that's how you feel."

"I guess I'll start looking for rings then."

We've left the restaurant, and I'm going to Olivia's apartment to drop her off. Spirits are high, in Olivia's case, it's alcohol induced. For me though, it's the love in the air. Not to say I'm already in love with this girl or anything like that, I'm not crazy, but there's something intoxicating about new love. The start of a new relationship, it's sort of the same feeling I got on move-in day last week. It's something new, something fresh, and in this case with

Olivia, something fun. Right now in this moment, I feel the way you feel after it's been raining for a week straight and it finally stops, and a rainbow appears. It's a dangerous feeling, because I know that anything that has the power to make me feel so good, has the power to make me feel miserable too. I think back to how gutted I felt when Jade ended things with me. How I felt looking at those flowers every day. I really hope things don't go that way with Olivia.

"God, I love day drinking. I'm feeling good." It doesn't seem like Olivia's fully drunk, but she's at least a little buzzed. We're at her apartment now, standing outside of her door.

"Yeah, me too, that water really hit the spot."

"Oh, shut up," says Olivia. She gives me a playful shove, but her hand lingers on my chest. We're so close that I can smell the flowery scent of her shampoo. Her deep green eyes gaze up at me expectantly, her lips are slightly parted, seemingly inviting me in.

The kiss is slightly different than the ones I had with Jade, but the sensation is equally satisfying. We remain interlocked for a few minutes before pulling apart when we hear someone climbing the stairs nearby.

Olivia blushes. "That was nice. You're a good kisser."

"Thank you," I say with a cheesy grin that always seems to appear on my face after I kiss someone.

"So, do you want to come in?"

I hesitate for a second before answering. "I would, but I promised Tristan I would meet him at the library today."

Olivia looks slightly disappointed. "Oh, uhh, okay then. Well I had a nice time with you. Make sure you hit me up to hang again soon."

"Yeah I had a good time too. I'll definitely hit you up soon."

I go back to my dorm feeling pretty good about myself. Overall, the date went well. I don't actually have plans with Tristan today, and even if I did, he would happily cancel them if he knew it meant I got to spend more time with a girl in a private space. But while I definitely feel like I've grown since my dates with Jade, I know I'm not yet ready for whatever awaits me inside Olivia's apartment. The thought of being alone with a girl in her room kind of stresses me out. I am still a virgin after all. That being said, it was certainly a step in the right direction. Hopefully my virgin status will soon be behind me.

THE BREAK-UP

"So, she invited you into her apartment and you said no?"

It's Tuesday, a couple of days after my date with Olivia. I'm sitting in the student union doing homework with Camryn, doing a play by play of the date. The student union became one of my favorite places to go to do work, or just hangout my first couple of years on campus. The student union is a pretty popular spot. Five floors of dining places, including the school store, a mini grocery store, and even a movie theater that plays movies that have been out of the actual movie theaters for a while. During the day, like most other places on campus, it's bustling. Full of life and energy, filled to the brim with students in a hurry to make it to their next class or waiting in line to get food from one of the dining areas.

At night though, it's quiet, barely anyone is there and it's easy to find a seat in a remote area. The ideal place for a natural wallflower such as myself to go to get work done. The library is nice too, but it's usually pretty crowded, so after eight o'clock during the week the student union is my sanctuary.

"I like her, but I don't know, it just felt like too much too soon."

"Interesting. I thought all guys lived for chances like that."

"Sure, maybe the guys who aren't twenty year old virgins with anxiety issues," I say bitterly.

My inexperience makes me feel anxious, which in turn makes becoming more experienced difficult, which makes me even more anxious. In the same way that social situations make me feel sweaty and uncomfortable, which ends up making me even more sweaty and uncomfortable. It's a vicious cycle that's funny to me in a way that's actually not at all funny, but instead super ironic and cruel.

"I just keep thinking about how if I suck in bed, everything will be over. I'll be so embarrassed."

"Yeah I get it, I remember being super nervous before my first time. I imagine there's even more pressure for a guy who's in college," says Camryn.

"Yeah exactly. Also, thank you for the advice you gave me before the date. Olivia loved everything you suggested."

Camryn laughs. "Why do you sound so surprised? You don't think I understand what women like?"

"I don't know, it was just crazy to me. You should start a dating advice service, like Will Smith in *Hitch.*"

"Better yet, maybe I should just take her out myself so she can get all of this first hand," Camryn says with a shrug.

"Chill chill, you know I can't compete against you. Does this mean you're officially on the market though?"

Camryn sighs. "Not yet, but I think I'm going to officially end things some time soon. I've written down my "breakup speech" and I'm just trying to mentally prepare."

"How do you feel about it?"

"I mean I guess I'm okay. It's not like he's done anything bad to me or anything. Really though, I don't think I'll know how I feel until after it happens."

"Well if you need to talk about it, just let me know. I feel like I owe you."

"Owe me? For what?"

"Uhh, for what? Have you not noticed all the help you've given me over the past few months. It's time I return the favor."

Camryn rolls her eyes. "Friends don't keep tabs on favors. It's not a game to see who can score the most friend points. And besides, you've done a lot for me too. I'd be lost here without you and Tristan."

At the mention of Tristan's name, her facial expression changes. It's hard for me to read, it reminds me of the guilty expression I had seen on Tristan's face a few days ago. I wonder what happened between them. "I just feel like we talk about me way more than we talk about you," I say, while shoving those thoughts aside.

"That's what friends are for."

As a kid I learned about ticks, these little spider-like things that bury themselves into your skin and suck the blood out of you, sometimes carrying various diseases. Sometimes I think I'm one of those ticks. There's a part of me, a big part of me, that feels unworthy of love. Not just romantic love, but platonic love too. I latch onto people like Camryn and Tristan knowing I can never give them back as much as they give me. Sometimes I think I'm just selfish and weak. All I can do is take from people. Look at how much Camryn has helped me with Jade, with Olivia, with life. And I've given her nothing in return except the occasionally sarcastic remark. I'm not worthy of her friendship. Once Camryn sees this, I'm sure she'll leave me behind, and maybe it's for the best. Maybe I deserve to be alone. That's probably why I've had so little success with women in the past. Nobody needs a tick or a leech like me in their life.

It's Thursday, a couple of weeks after the meetup with Camryn at the student union, and I hear a knock on my door. Tristan walks in. Our schedules have been so hectic that I've basically not seen him at all since the group dinner at the dining hall during the first week of classes.

"Hey man," says Tristan.

"Hey, what's up?"

"Nothing, I just feel like we've barely seen each other since the semester started. Also, I was thinking, we should go on a double date. Me and Liz, with you and Olivia."

"How do you know that me and Olivia are even still a thing? For all you know she could have killed my dog or something."

"You don't have a dog," says Tristan pointedly. "Are you saying you and Olivia aren't on good terms anymore?"

"We are actually. We've been facetiming a lot, and we've been meeting up at the library almost every day. "

"Oooh you've been facetiming," Tristan says in a sing-songy voice.

"Shut up," I say, trying to suppress a grin. "It's just one of those things, you know? The beginning stages when you want to talk to someone all the time."

"Yeah, no, I've never experienced that I don't think."

"What about with Liz? You've never felt that way about her?"

Tristan sighs. "I don't know, it's just not what I thought it'd be with her. Sometimes I think I'm just destined to feel this apathy towards women and relationships. Before this, I thought it was because Liz messed me up so much, but now, I don't know. I just feel cursed."

After all the times Tristan's been there for me, I'm determined to be there for him. Determined not to feel like a tick anymore. "Okay, so the double date?"

"Yeah, I'm hoping that it can spark something that makes me feel the way I think I should feel with Liz. I know it's far-fetched, but I mean I might as well try it."

"You know I'm down, let me just check with Olivia."

"A double date with Tristan and his girlfriend?"

It's Friday night. Olivia and I are walking around campus after dinner, and I've just brought up the idea for a double date that Tristan had last night.

"Well I don't think Liz is Tristan's girlfriend officially right now, but yeah that's the idea pretty much."

"I don't know, I've heard things about Tristan," says Olivia.

"You've heard things? What kind of things?"

"Well a friend told me, that one of her friends told her, about how Tristan is a pig that just uses girls for sex and then never calls them back."

"Tristan's had his hoe phases, but he's a good guy once you get to know him."

"You're just saying that because he's your friend."

"Okay, yes, Tristan and I have been friends for as long as I can remember, so obviously I'm going to be a little biased when it comes to him, but I really think you'll like him."

At that moment I feel my phone buzzing in my pocket. I've programmed my phone so it only goes off if certain people call, otherwise it goes straight to voicemail, so I know it must be important. I take it out of my pocket, and see that it's Camryn calling.

"Is it cool if I take this? It's Camryn." Olivia looks somewhat displeased, but she nods.

"Hey, what's up?"

"Hey, Roman, do you think we can talk? Like in person?" Her voice sounds different, it doesn't have its usual sharpness. Also it could just be my imagination, but do I hear sniffling?

"I'm with Olivia right now. What's up? Are you okay?"

There's a brief pause. "Oh, no it's okay then, we can talk about it some other time."

"No, no it's cool. I'm kind of far from your dorm, but we can meet by the fountain in the quad if that's okay with you."

"Yeah, okay that works."

"Cool, I'll be there in like 20 minutes."

As I hang up the phone my mind starts racing. Camryn's never called me, and asked to see me like that before. I wonder what it could be about? But, first thing's first, I have to somehow break the news to Olivia that I need to leave her to be with another girl.

"So, you're leaving."

"I—yeah, I'm sorry, it's just Camryn. It sounds like she needs to talk about something that's kind of serious. But have you decided on the double date yet? "

Olivia sighs. "Okay, I'll come on the double date." She gives me a look that tells me I may regret my decision to go talk to Camryn, but if I ignore my friends when they need me, then I'll really be no better than the leech I tell myself I am. I have to prove to myself that I'm not a selfish, worthless asshole.

Similar to the student union, the quad is normally pretty busy, but on Friday night all the people who would normally be here during the day, are off planning their weekend activities. When I find Camryn, I'm completely caught off guard. She's off by herself, and she's crying. Her normal glamorous, put together appearance is nowhere to be found. I've never seen her look more vulnerable. I recall how strong and proud she was when we first met, like a tiger waiting to attack. Now she may as well be a helpless kitten who's lost her way.

"Hey, what happened?" I ask as I cautiously approach the bench she's sitting on.

"Justin and I broke up—or I guess I should say, he broke up with me."

"I'm sorry to hear that. I know how much he meant to you at one point."

"Yeah, it's just when you're with someone for so long, it's hard to picture yourself without them," says Camryn as she tries to wipe away her tears. "I didn't think it'd hurt this much because it's pretty much been over for a few weeks, but I guess I was just holding out hope that things would end up getting worked out."

Camryn and I have been friends for a few months now, but as far as physical contact is concerned, we may as well be distant cousins who occasionally give each other awkward side hugs. Normally I feel extremely self conscious around her, partially because of my natural social awkwardness, partially because I don't want to cross any boundaries as her friend. There seems to be this invisible barrier that I'm afraid of crossing with her that inevitably leads to me catching feelings, which then leads to me helplessly watching those feelings get shot down like they always seem to. Those thoughts and fears seem unimportant to me right now though. I feel this surge of protectiveness as I look at her in this somber, vulnerable state. Instinctively I move closer to her, and put my arm around her in a comforting manner. She lays her head on my chest, and I feel her lean her body weight into me as if she just broke her leg, and I'm her crutch.

I try to think of things to say to her that can help, but I still haven't experienced what she's going through. The situation with Jade is the closest I've come to a breakup, and that relationship lasted all of two months. Somehow telling her that she should just go out and meet someone else doesn't seem like the right thing to say in this situation. But still, I desperately want to be there for her the way she has been there for me so many times.

"I remember how you were that night at the party. Are you afraid of being single?"

"I don't know, maybe. I've just been in a relationship for so long, you know?"

"Maybe this time when you're single will be good for you."

"Yeah, maybe you're right," Camryn says, looking unconvinced.

"When I'm feeling down, I like to fill the void in my heart with junk food. You want to go to Sonic or something? I'll pay for your food."

"Sure, why not," says Camryn.

In the past, whenever I felt down in the dumps, Tristan would take me somewhere to get food, usually Sonic. Sonic is by no means high end dining, but to me, that's part of its charm. Tristan and I would sit in the car, talking about whatever was bothering me, eating the trashy fast food that manages to be as terrible for your body as it is good for the soul. Hopefully this strategy works with Camryn too.

We're parked at Sonic eating our food. I get a cookie dough blast, and Camryn has an Oreo blast. We also got a large order of mozzarella sticks that we're sharing. The song "Crack Rock" by Frank Ocean is playing in the background.

"So...Sonic? Seems like a random place to pig out on junk food," says Camryn, whose mood seems to have improved once she started eating her food.

"Yeah yeah yeah. It seems to be working, so I don't know why you're complaining. Would you rather we went to Mcdonald's?"

"I guess you're right. These mozzarella sticks are worth the trip for sure."

"Yeah I can tell you like them, you've eaten like the whole bag."

Camryn laughs. You can still see the residual effects of her tears, her eyes are still red and puffy, she's still sniffling, but it's good to see her spirits starting to rise again. "So how did Olivia take it when you told her you were coming to see me?"

"Oh she seemed very happy about it. Not at all disappointed in any way," I say sarcastically. I don't want you to worry about that though. Tonight is about you."

Camryn sighs, putting her head in her hands. "You didn't have to come, you know. I would've understood."

"What are you talking about? Of course I had to come. That's what friends do," I say with a shrug. "Sometimes I feel unworthy of your friendship. It feels good to be the one to give instead of take for once."

"One of the reasons I wanted to transfer, outside of Justin, was to make new friends. I felt like my friends weren't there enough for me. Fighting all those battles by yourself takes a toll eventually. I guess that's why I always made sure to help you with Jade over the summer, I wanted to be for you what I wanted for myself. If that makes sense. I guess I'm trying to say I'm used to my friends not showing up for me."

"Well I'll always make sure to show up for you."

We finish up our food, and head back to campus. As I sit there in the driver's seat, feeling my heart rate accelerate because of all the sugar I just ate, I feel a sense of pride. It's the way I felt when I was the one to hit the game winning shot in a middle school playoff game instead of Tristan. I was able to help someone, and help myself in the process. For once I was able to quiet one of the demons in my head that always tries to denigrate me.

I pull up to Camryn's dorm to drop her off. Before getting out, she turns to me and says, "Roman, thank you so much for being there. I appreciate this more than you know." Maybe I'm not so worthless after all.

THE ULTIMATUM

One thing I've liked about the dynamic with Olivia has been how open she seems to be with me. I haven't had to doubt whether or not she likes me, but after leaving her to console Camryn, things have seemed different. Once I got back to my dorm, after seeing Camryn, I texted Olivia to make sure everything was good, but she was pretty short with me. I have this feeling in the pit of my stomach that's similar to the feeling you get when you're outside right before it rains. It's how I imagine Spider-Man feels when his spider sense goes off. In his case, it's a sense of when a villain is about to attack. For me though, it's a sense of when a girl stops liking me.

I think about calling Camryn to talk about it. A week ago if I was having trouble with Olivia, I'd definitely call her, but now it feels like I shouldn't. I don't want her to feel any guilt over the situation, which is silly because she did nothing wrong. I guess I could try to talk to Tristan about it, but he doesn't give the best advice in situations like this. He'd probably just tell me to dump

Olivia for Camryn or something. Times like these make me wish I had more friends.

Eventually I decided to watch a movie. I put on *Thor Ragnarok,* which was a Christmas present from Tristan. Watching Thor build himself up after being torn down is inspiring to me. In moments where I'm feeling kind of weak or uncertain, it's nice to see someone overcome their own weaknesses to be great. It's one of the reasons I want to write my own graphic novel, so I can feel that experience vicariously through my own character.

Halfway through the scene where Thor and Hulk fight, I hear a knock on my door, and Tristan comes in.

"You ready for today?" he asks, casually leaning on the door frame. "Oh, you're watching Ragnarok? That movie is sick. That reminds me. How is your comic coming?"

Outside of the comic club that I'm in, Tristan and Camryn are still the only ones that know about my dreams of creating my own graphic novel. For some reason I always get really touchy about the subject. Talking about it with other people usually leads to a lot of questions that I don't want to answer. It reminds me of the first day or two after scraping my knee as a kid, when the wound is still fresh and any slight poke leads to discomfort. Talking about it with Tristan and Camryn doesn't make me feel that way though, probably because they're the only two people who I've felt this type of closeness with.

"Yeah, I'm ready. Olivia confirmed that she's ready to go. My comic is going well I think, I don't know. I have to submit it by September 30th to qualify, so we'll see how it goes."

I try to seem laid back when talking about it, but my passion for the project leaps out of my pores like smoke from a boiling tea kettle. Tristan sees this and laughs.

"I love seeing that look in your eye when you talk about something that's important to you, it's how you looked the first time you told me about that mystery girl you met in the quad. It's also the look you got that time I beat you in bowling."

"Yeah well, don't get too cocky, I'm definitely beating you in mini golf today.

Tristan laughs again. "We'll see about that."

The minigolf place has 18 holes, each one with different plastic animal replicas, that serve as obstacles, along with the occasional windmill. There's very little tension in the air, which I'm pleasantly surprised by. Olivia and Liz get along right away, and start chattering about the show *You*, a show that just recently came out on Netflix, and the genius behind the Joe Goldberg character.

"I think there's something so interesting about the subversion of the nice guy trope," says Liz as she lines up her first shot. Liz is close to my complexion with goddess braids that go a little bit past her shoulders. Like most girls that Tristan goes after, she's undeniably pretty.

"Yeah, I've always felt that guys that like to label themselves as "nice guys" are trying to convince themselves as much as they're trying to convince you. A real nice guy doesn't have to say they're nice, or a good person. Like Roman," says Olivia while shifting her gaze to me.

I've always looked at the "nice guy" label as the kiss of death. Something people say when they don't know what other good things to say. Like when someone says a girl has a good personality. Not to say it's not true, but for example, no one calls Tristan a nice guy. I think he's nice, but if I were to describe him I wouldn't give him that label, and that's because it's not needed. He has other positive traits that people can latch onto. Being labeled as nice is a shallow accomplishment at best.

"Personally I think the whole nice guy discourse is crap," says Tristan as he sinks a shot. "Girls say they like guys who are nice, so guys pretend to be nice to get girls. But what does it mean to be nice anyway? I could be the worst guy in the world to everyone except my girl, and she might call me a nice guy, but does that make me nice? It's all just a matter of perception really."

"I guess you're right, but I still think Joe Goldberg's an interesting character," says Liz with a shrug. "A man driven crazy by love. To the point that he's willing to stalk women and make himself out to be the perfect guy for them."

I think about the similarities between Joe Goldberg and myself. Obviously his character is meant to be a satirical, dramatic, exaggeration but he's based on a real world trope. I've looked through girl's social media pages in the past, to see what we have in common, which I guess is a lesser version of what Joe does in the show. In a way I'm no better than him, trying to make myself into the perfect guy. I guess really it comes down to my own insecurities, not thinking my authentic self is enough, and feeling the urge to mask my real self from outsiders. It's probably why I feel so uncomfortable showing people my graphic novel too. My graphic novel is a small piece of my authentic self in art form, and any potential reveal and rejection of my authentic self is too painful to bear. Maybe that's what Camryn and Tristan mean when they say I need to tap into my super power, my authentic self. After all, Olivia was attracted to the real version of me, there was no way for me to mask myself, and things are going pretty well.

But it's hard, almost impossible really. It's become popular for people to say they're fighting their demons, but for me they're very real. They live in my head and manifest as dark thoughts that come in randomly, loudly, persistently. It's like wearing invisible airpods that just tell you how much of a loser you are constantly every day. The way things ended with Jade certainly didn't help matters, but maybe Olivia will help me quiet down the voices to some extent.

We're halfway through the course now, and somehow our team is in the lead. Similar to the bowling double date we went on over the summer, we split ourselves up into two teams. Olivia and I, against Tristan and Liz. Once Tristan told me where he wanted to go for the double date, I started watching YouTube videos about how to best swing a golf club. It's safe to say I'm as much of a golf master as you can be in three days with only a video guide without any actual practice. It may just be a game of mini golf, but I'm ready to finally beat Tristan at something. It may have turned out well with Jade after that bowling loss, but seeing Tristan's smug expression every time I lose to him, takes its toll. For years, I've felt like his sidekick. A victory over him not only would help temporarily quiet the negative voices in my head, but after years of feeling inferior, it would serve as a landmark moment that helps to symbolize that I'm ready to elevate to his level.

After eleven holes, we're up by six strokes. Luckily for me it turns out that Olivia is pretty good at minigolf. We're more than halfway through the game, if we can just maintain the lead, I'll finally have my win over Tristan. I can feel the anticipation coursing through my body like electricity. Olivia goes, and makes the shot in seven strokes, I go up and make the shot in five strokes. We're in good shape.

"So how did you guys meet?" asks Liz as Tristan tries to hit his ball into the plastic alligator's mouth.

"A friend of his came up to me at a party and asked for my number on his behalf. He had this whole dark, brooding, mysterious thing going for him. And he had a woman put in a good word for him, which I saw as a good sign, so I gave her my number to give to him," says Olivia.

It's funny to me how a lot of my social anxiety driven habits come across as mysterious to other people. I'm sure it'd seem less cool if they knew what was going through my mind in those moments.

"That's sweet. I know a lot of women are insecure about guys having friends that are girls, so it's cool of you to not care about something like that," says Liz.

"Camryn seemed cool, and I trust Roman so I'm not worried about it," says Olivia. "Plus she has a long term boyfriend."

"Oh, actually her and her boyfriend broke up," I say feeling kind of annoyed with myself for forgetting to tell Olivia. I glance over at Olivia and find that she's giving me a look that's similar to the one she gave me the night I left her to go to Camryn, disappointment.

"Really? They broke up?" asks Tristan as he walks over to us after finally getting his ball into the hole. His facial expression is hard to read. Like the look you get when you get a callback about a job you thought you'd gotten rejected from after you've already started working somewhere else. If Liz wasn't here, and if I wasn't so focused on beating him, I'd probably question him about it, "Did she say why?"

"She said they were just growing apart," I say as I go to get ready for my turn.

"So that's why she called you the other day." Olivia says quietly, her facial expression escalating from disappointment to perturbance.

I try to put my focus back on the minigolf game, but from there it goes downhill. Our team mojo is thrown completely off wack. The energy in the air between Olivia and I changes. I can feel her annoyance without her saying a word. The pressure in the air feels like it's increased tenfold, the way it does when you're in an airplane, or driving in high elevation. My focus is gone. My confidence is shot. All of the advice I had received from the golfing tutorials I watched have been erased from my brain.

After the last hole, we ended up losing by three strokes. Another loss to Tristan, and now Olivia's clearly upset with me too.

We're going back to Olivia's dorm to drop her off. The car ride has been uncomfortably quiet with the exception of the music I was playing. I had made it a rule to always have one of my playlists or a podcast playing at all times while I'm driving, perfect for times like now when I'm feeling on edge.

Before she gets out, Olivia focuses her gaze on mine. "Do you have feelings for Camryn?"

"No, we're just friends," I answered honestly.

"I know we're not like, *together* together yet, but I really don't want to get involved with another man who has an attachment to a woman they say is just a friend, but is really more. That's what happened with my ex, and he ended up cheating on me with her," Olivia says bitterly.

"Camryn and I are just friends. Really. I mean I wouldn't be with you right now if not for her."

"I get that. It was cool of her to approach me like she did at that party, but things change when one of the people in a friendship becomes single. She's feeling vulnerable, she needs a shoulder to cry on, and then there you are. Her knight in shining armor. That's how feelings start to develop."

"I don't know what you want me to say. I'm her friend. Since I've known her, she's always been there for me. It was time for me to return the favor."

"Look Roman, I'm going to cut to the chase. I don't think this is going to work out unless you keep your distance from Camryn. At least for a while," says Olivia, sharply.

"So, what? I'm supposed to just stop talking to her? She needs me. She doesn't really have any friends here yet."

"You can text her occasionally, but I don't want you guys hanging out in person. I don't know what else to say. It's her or me," says Olivia as she goes to get out of the car. "I like you, Roman, but I can't go through another situation like the one with my ex."

I forget to play music as I drive back to my dorm. I'm too distracted by the bomb Olivia dropped on me to adhere to silly rules I'd made up. I don't have many friends. Camryn's been better to me than I ever could have imagined. When it comes to friends, I have a habit of not letting people get close to me, and then dropping at the first opportunity, but I don't want to leave a friend like Camryn behind. Especially now, when she needs me the most. But I don't know, I really like Olivia, or at least I did. Maybe that's just the kind of sacrifice it takes to find love.

Olivia's Interlude

From a young age, Olivia was forced to compete in beauty pageants. It's not like she hated them, it wasn't her choice to participate, but it wasn't the worst thing. As the oldest child, she was a natural people pleaser, and making her parents proud by doing something they wanted her to do made her happy. However, this led to her seeking validation from others. Years of being scrutinized by judges, led to her teen years being ravaged by her insecurities. She craved male attention and validation, which caused her to jump from relationship to relationship in the early stages of her high school life. Finally she met Andy. Olivia always wanted to be one of those people that got married young to their high school sweetheart, and after two years, she thought she was well on her way. She'd finally found stability. That is, until Andy cheated on her with the girl he claimed was his best friend. When things with Andy ended, it caused her to go on a tailspin, her insecurities at an all time high. That's why when she came across Roman, a seemingly nice, cute, harmless guy who poured all of the attention she desired into her, she was ecstatic. But once she saw Camryn coming into the picture, it triggered her. Causing her insecurities and paranoia to flare up all over again.

THE PREGAME

It's Saturday, almost a week from when Olivia gave me the ultimatum. I've tried to avoid both Olivia and Camryn all week, not having the guts to make a decision. It should be easy, after all Olivia is exactly what I've been wanting. At least I thought she was. She's pretty, she's easy to talk to, and she actually seems to like me. What more could I want? But when she gave me the ultimatum, it got me thinking. If things with Olivia are really meant to be, would I really have to cut off a good friend to be with her?

If this were a movie, this would be the scene where the main character realizes that the woman they thought was just a friend, is who they were meant to be with all along. I try to look within myself to see how I'm feeling but my emotions are all jumbled. It's so confusing. Camryn and I have become close over the past few months. We didn't necessarily click right away, I don't think we're a match made in heaven, but I've never met anyone who's put in as much effort to get to know me as she has. I feel comfortable around her, which I can't say for a lot of people, especially not women who I find attractive. Is that a sign that we're destined to be together? At first, the thing holding back any potential feelings was her relationship. Now though, there's no restriction. I've never been able to be just friends with a woman who's single before, but I've also never been as close to a woman as I am with Camryn. That being said, just because we're close doesn't mean she even wants to be with me in that way. Maybe this whole internal conflict is being wasted on a girl who only ever wanted to be friends.

I know if I told Camryn about the ultimatum, she would say all the right things. That she understands where Olivia is coming from. That she would be okay handling the breakup on her own. But at this point, I've known her long enough to know that she would say or do whatever was necessary to make sure she didn't block one of her friends from something they wanted. In this case she knows how much it would mean to me to have this relationship with Olivia work out.

But what kind of friend would I be to cut Camryn off just to be with Olivia? I imagine I'd feel pretty dumb if I end up getting dumped by Olivia and then try to go back to being friends with Camryn, like nothing changed. Like that episode in *Seinfeld* when George quits his job and then later tries to come back after realizing he can't find another job, and then pretends like nothing happened. It's hard to forget someone choosing someone else over you so blatantly. I don't see how we could ever bounce back from that.

Rejection isn't new to me. Sasha, Jade, and many others have used me as their personal punching bag. I don't know if things with Olivia will end any differently than it did with those other girls, but I do know that what I have with Camryn is rare. At least for me. But at the same time, finding love has always been the goal. This is the closest I've come to finding something real. Jade and Olivia have both seemed like extremely lucky situations for me. Like the universe was trying to repay me for years of being buried by various different romantic interests. But what if this is my last shot at cashing in on that luck?

As I'm contemplating this thought, I hear a knock on my door. Tristan comes in. "You ready for the tailgate today?"

Earlier in the week Tristan convinced me to go with him to the tailgate. Before every home football game, there's this big tailgate outside the stadium that's basically just a big party. More people go to the tailgate than to the actual game. There are different tents set up, with loud music playing and an endless supply of alcohol. It's not exactly my scene, but I figured it was a good way to get my mind off of things for a while. Plus I haven't had a chance to hang out with Tristan much, so it was a hard offer to turn down.

"Yeah, I'm ready whenever," I say.

"Cool, we can head over to DJ's place in like twenty minutes."

I wasn't stoked to have to go to the tailgate with Dalton, and even less stoked that we had to go to his place beforehand, because his apartment is off campus. He always keeps his place stocked up on alcohol though, so Tristan likes to go there first to pregame before functions. Camryn isn't coming with us today because she said she had to study for some test. Which I have mixed feelings about. Happy because I could continue putting off the whole ultimatum stuff with Olivia, and upset because for the past month and a half since the semester started, she served as a perfect balance to Dalton's aggravating behavior. It's the first tailgate I'll have gone to since last year though, so I'm kind of excited. I think it'll be a good day.

We knock on the door to Dalton's place, and after a moment or two, his roommate answers the door. His roommate, Charles, is also on the basketball team. He plays center, and he's close to seven feet tall. I always hate when I have to look up to people.

"What's up guys," says Charles. "DJ has a girl over right now. He'll be out in a minute."

We go to sit down on their couch. As upperclassmen, Tristan and I have a pretty nice dorm, one of the nicer ones on campus, but Charles and Dalton's apartment is considerably bigger and nicer than our dorm. They have a nice bar area near the kitchen with high chairs, a leather sofa with matching leather chairs in the living room area, and a fancy flat screen tv connected to a sound system that's playing music.

"I think we need to live off campus next year," says Tristan as he takes in the room.

I continue looking around the room, they have a pretty nice setup. As I'm looking around, I see a pink lanyard with a set of keys, pepper spray, and a whistle attached to it on one of the recliner chairs in the living room. I'm guessing it belongs to the girl Dalton's with, because most guys don't go around with pink lanyards with pepper spray. Next to the lanyard is a wallet with a sticker on it. I squint to see what the sticker is, for some reason transfixed by this anomaly in what's otherwise your typical male apartment setup. The sticker looks to be a singer with blonde hair. I go through my internal rolodex to think of singers with blonde hair. What kind of college aged girl goes around with stickers of pop stars on their wallets anyway? That's when it all clicked for me. Hannah Montana, the only girl I know who carries around Hannah Montana stickers is Olivia. Surely it must be a coincidence though. I must have come across the only other girl at this school who has the same affinity for old Disney stars. All doubt leaves my mind, however, when seconds later Dalton's door opens and I see a girl with shocking red hair, and an oversized t-shirt that I'm guessing belonged to Dalton, walk out. It's Olivia.

Olivia turns her attention towards me, her face full of surprise. "Oh, Roman, I didn't think you'd be here."

That's when Dalton walks out behind her, shirtless. "Oh, damn. I didn't think y'all would get here so early."

As I realize what's going on, I feel my insides start to burn. As if a fire had been lit in my stomach, that was slowly getting bigger and bigger. I notice Tristan beside me, his mouth agape, momentarily too shocked to move. My pupils start to dilate, I can feel the adrenaline coursing through my body like water through a hose when the nozzle is turned all the way on. My rage consumes me. The music from the speakers that was just a second ago playing so loud that I could barely hear myself think, is mere background noise. My heart pounds vigorously, as if I just got done running sprints.

"Wait, Roman chill out," I hear Tristan say faintly in the background. He's come to his senses, but I'm too far gone to take in his words. All of my focus is on Dalton. We may not have been friends, but he knew Olivia and I were a thing. He broke the code. Before I can think of a more rational, diplomatic solution, I find myself standing, my fists clenched as if I'm in the ring with Mike Tyson. All I can see is red, completely and utterly mesmerized by my desire for vengeance. I'm hungry for blood, Dalton's blood.

I go to make a move, but before I can take a full step, Tristan grabs me and takes me outside. While Tristan is a D1 basketball player, years of relentless weight training have made me strong. Normally he's not as strong as I am, but while I thrash against him, trying to get free, his grip somehow remains firm. Finally I give up, my chest heaving from the rush of adrenaline.

"Roman, I know you're upset, but you've gotta calm down. You're supposed to be the chill one here," says Tristan.

I'm briefly reminded of all the times I've had to bail Tristan out of heated situations. The time he almost got kicked out of a playoff game in high school. The time he got into it with a football player at the school rec center during a game of pickup basketball. The time he tried to challenge the whole rugby club to a fight because they were charging us to get into a party. Now I was the one getting into a reckless situation, and he was the one bailing me out. "Listen, I can't have you flying off the rails like that. It'll throw our whole dynamic out of whack. We can't both be hotheads."

"I get that, but Dalton deserves it," I say, hardly recognizing the sound of my own voice. All of my adrenaline and anger causes my voice, which is normally soft and even keeled, to be significantly more forceful and aggressive. It's hard going through life feeling and sounding so timid, but I hate how out of control my rage makes me feel.

"Yeah, I'm going to talk to him about it. That was really fucked up."

"He literally knew we were a thing. I don't understand why he'd do this," I say, my voice tinged with defeat. I guess I should be used to this. I've been getting rejected and overlooked in favor of guys like Dalton my whole life. I don't know why I thought it'd be different with Olivia. I think back to the dinner a few weeks ago when Dalton had said that Olivia was in one of his classes. How long has he been going after her?

We leave Dalton's apartment and go back to our dorm. I feel kind of guilty because instead of going to the tailgate, Tristan decides to stay with me. I tell him he can go without me, but he insists that he doesn't want me to be alone, and Camryn is still studying. We ordered a pizza and put on an episode of *Parks and Rec,* one of my comfort shows. Normally we'd put on some sort of superhero show or movie, but in more extreme cases, such as this one with Olivia and Dalton, *Parks and Rec* is the show I turn to. The last time we had a situation as dire as this one was the Sasha incident. Tristan and I ended up pulling an all-nighter watching old *Parks and Rec* episodes the night the embarrassing screenshot was posted on Twitter. *Parks and Rec* is the perfect show for me to watch when I'm on the verge of a depressive episode. It's relatively light hearted, but still manages to entertain me. The April character reminds me of myself in some ways. The cold, socially awkward, introvert who is secretly soft hearted, is a characterization that hits close to home for me.

My mind wanders to Olivia. This whole time I've been getting upset at Dalton, when Olivia is just as guilty. How could she choose to be with a guy as sleezy as Dalton instead of me? And to think I was really considering choosing her over Camryn. I guess I should be thankful for that situation today, it saved me from making the wrong decision.

"So how are things with you and Liz?" I ask hoping for good news.

Tristan sighs. "I ended things with her. It just wasn't what I was expecting. I think I might want someone else to be honest."

"Who? Is it someone I know?"

"Yeah, but it's probably better if I didn't say right now."

Tristan's never spoken this way about a girl before. He's not the type to pine over someone the way that I have so many times in the past (and the present). Usually if he likes a girl, he just goes for it, and usually gets them. I briefly consider the notion that the girl he has feelings for might be the same mystery girl that I currently share a class with. It would explain why he's so hesitant to tell me. I try to brush this thought to the side. If I can't compete with Dalton, there's no way I can compete with Tristan over a girl, and I don't think I can take that right now.

"Olivia wanted me to stop talking to Camryn. She was worried that I'd catch feelings for her or something like that."

"You weren't seriously considering that right?" Tristan asks, more defensively than I was expecting.

"Uhh I don't know. I mean Camryn's a great friend, but you know I've been looking for something more for a while."

Tristan directs his gaze away from the TV, directly at me. "Okay, I get that, but Camryn is loyal, clever, and she has her shit together. You need someone like her in your life. Haven't you ever considered her as something more than a friend?"

The truth was that I'd been obsessed over the answer to that question all week, but no way could I let Tristan know that. Obviously I have to play it cool, at least for now, when I'm still so uncertain about my feelings. On paper it seems like we make a good match, but that's not saying a lot.

"The stuff with Olivia got me thinking about it, but I don't know. Even if I did like her in that way, it's not like it's a guarantee that she feels the same way," I say while grabbing another slice of the meat lover's stuffed crust pizza.

Tristan averts his gaze, wearing the same expression on his face that he's been showing the last few weeks whenever Camryn's brought up. "Maybe it'd be worth the risk," he mutters, almost as if he's talking to himself.

It's Monday, a couple of days after the tailgate incident. I hate saying I feel depressed, because it's become almost like a popular quirk to say you're depressed, but I still feel this lingering extreme sadness about the events that took place over the weekend. The overwhelming rage I felt, has all converted to sadness and angst. I call out of my internship and skip my classes for the day. Too embarrassed to show my face, even though it's extremely unlikely that anyone I'd run into would even know what happened. My pride is battered, and my heart is hurt. I muster enough energy to go get a snack from our mini kitchen area, and I see Tristan sitting on the couch in our living room, icing his hand.

"Hey, I'm surprised to see you here. Aren't you supposed to be at practice?"

"Aren't you supposed to be at your internship?" Tristan asks.

"I'm taking a personal day," I say while grabbing a pack of peanut butter crackers.

"Yeah, well, I guess I am too in a way," says Tristan with a bitter laugh. "I had a talk with our boy DJ today. It ended with me punching him in the face in front of the coaches. They sent me home early, and suspended me for the first game of the season."

I avert my gaze, looking down at the floor. "I...I don't know what to say. You didn't have to do all that for me."

"Of course I did," Tristan says definitively. "You didn't think I'd let him get away with that did you? Just because I didn't want you to punch him, doesn't mean I can't. It's partially my fault for always bringing him around anyway."

"I'm grateful, but you gotta be more careful. You could've gotten kicked off the team."

"Oh, please. They need me out there, I'm the team captain. It was about time someone knocked some sense into DJ anyway. He may be my teammate, but you and I are brothers."

I meant it when I said I was grateful for Tristan. Reckless violence suits his personality more than mine. We've always been like fire and ice. Without my ice, Tristan's fire would explode, burning everything down in the process. Without Tristan's fire I would be frozen, stuck in place, never evolving. Me lecturing Tristan after he goes and does something crazy, that's the way things should be. I feel my anger and sadness start to lessen as the universe returns to the natural order of things.

THE GROUP PROJECT

In the weeks that followed the Olivia and Dalton incident, I kept a low profile. As an introvert, I'm already a natural homebody, but I've gone even further in that direction the past few weeks. I've been in a haze, like I'm living my life with some kind of fog permanently surrounding me. I don't feel upset at Olivia or Dalton, I don't feel happy going to the gym or working on my graphic novel. Mostly I just feel nothingness. This profound emptiness in the pit of my stomach, and in my chest where my heart should be. I've almost exclusively been going to my internship, to class, and to the gym. I even skipped my comic club meetings a few times. The same old routine, boring, monotonous, safe. I wonder if it's better to feel anger or sadness like I felt right after the Olivia situation, or nothing at all like I feel now. Tristan would invite me out to do different things, but I'd almost always say no. Except when it was my birthday and it was time for the annual recurring nightmare for anyone with social anxiety, a party thrown in your honor.

"It's your 21st birthday. You have to go big for that one," Tristan had said. As someone who doesn't drink, my 21st birthday held little significance to me, and being around a big group of people who I knew mostly didn't even really care about me, didn't sound all that appealing to me. It's hard being Tristan's friend sometimes, especially in social settings. Watching everyone's face light up once they see him, and then fall once they see me. The night of my birthday was filled with that fake enthusiastic happy birthday greeting. Like the one you would give a classmate in middle school when the teacher announces it to the class, and you're just trying to be nice. And so, I found a way to leave early when all of the attention was mercifully off of me.

Whenever I'm out in a social setting, I feel as if I'm either being judged by everyone around me, or I'm being completely ignored. I realize now that I'm not meant to be the guy in the spotlight like Tristan or even Dalton. That's probably why every time I've tried to prove to myself that I'm more than I am, I get crushed. Like a bug. I wanted my chance to get in the game, to prove myself, but it's clear I belong on the sidelines.

The good news is that Camryn and I had continued our friendship without a hitch. Her and Tristan both did a lot to try to boost my spirits. Camryn had said that I have nothing to feel bad about, I did nothing wrong. While that may be true, I can't help but feel that I am the thing that's wrong, my personality, me as a person. These women keep getting to know me, and running in the opposite direction. The only logical explanation is that there's something wrong with me, and if I don't fix it, it'll just keep happening over and over again. I've spent so much time trying to find love or some kind of connection, but right now I just want to feel okay again.

I remember seeing a tweet a while ago that said how hard the dating game was, and at the time it didn't fully resonate because I hadn't even gotten past the first date stage by that point. So it was all kind of alien to me. In my mind, once someone likes you enough to go out with you a second time, that's it, it'll all work out. My time with Jade and Olivia showed me what the tweets meant. It took me so long to get past just the first hurdle, and now I see that the next hurdles I have to clear are even higher and more difficult to get past.

In my social psychology class, the mystery girl hasn't sat next to me again, and I still haven't talked to her. Maybe I never will, it's probably for the best. I don't even know what I would say to her. "Hey, I'm Roman, you may remember me as that weird guy who tried talking to you a few months ago. Well I'm here to say I have a massive crush on you. By the way, what's your name?" I'm sure she would laugh in my face. Every class I see her walk in, fashionably late, and every class without fail, I feel my heart skip a beat. She probably doesn't even know I exist, but that's part of her allure. There's just something about quiet, unassuming, girls who don't know I exist.

It's about halfway through the semester now, and the professor tells us about the project we'll be working on for the rest of the semester. A group project that ends with a presentation in front of the whole class, how fun. We'll have to organize our own study, and record the results in a research paper. The research paper has to include our hypothesis, an annotated bibliography with background on our study and why it's important, information on the study itself, and of course the results. It all sounds like it's going to be a shit ton of work. Nothing fills me with more dread than a presentation. You give me the option to either fight Thanos with all the infinity stones, or give a presentation in front of a group of people, I'm choosing the fight with Thanos every time. Being in front of people with all that attention on me? I shutter at the thought. Whenever I'm forced to do it, I get all sweaty, and my voice gets shaky. It's terrible. And now the mystery girl is in my class too, so I know she'll be there to see me at my absolute worst. Wonderful.

The professor goes on to tell the class that the groups are going to be randomly assigned, and we're supposed to sit with them during every class for the rest of the semester. Group projects for me are a mixed bag that's mostly mixed with bad. Your group mates are kind of like your coworkers, you're just a group of people forced to be around each other for a common cause. It makes the whole conversational dynamic awkward, you don't want to talk solely about the work at hand, but you're unsure of how much outside information to divulge. If you're a socially awkward guy like myself, you might just spend the whole class thinking of clever ways to insert yourself into the conversation, ultimately failing and not saying anything except the bare minimum. You try to work together to split up the work as evenly as possible, but there's always a slacker that the group has to make up for. Ultimately though, I kind of like group projects just because the pressure to perform isn't quite as high as working alone. Presenting with a group is still horrible, but not as unbearable as presenting by yourself.

The professor puts up the groups on the board, and there's a moment of chaos as everyone in the class tries to maneuver around and get themselves situated. This is probably the worst part of working in a group. The beginning, before you know who the people in your group actually are. I wander around like a lost dog, looking for the rest of my group. After several minutes of asking random people what their names are, I finally find where two of the three other members of my group are sitting. Aaron and Jack, they seem to be easy going guys. They remind me of some of the frat boys that Tristan and I have come across during some of our nights out. They're already talking with each other. That just leaves one more. According to the board that has all of our names on it, her name is Fiona. We're at the group forming stage where almost everyone's found their groups, and there are just a few stragglers left over. Curiously enough, one of the stragglers is the mystery girl, who I sat next to on the first day of class, and made a fool of myself in front of a few months ago before summer break.

I'm conflicted. Do I want her to be in my group for this project? It would give me an excuse to talk to her, and I could finally stop referring to her as "mystery girl" in my head, but I feel confident that if she is in my group, I will find a way to make a fool of myself...again. Or even worse, she'll end up having sex with Dalton like Olivia did, or falling in love with Tristan like half of my high school crushes did. I'm probably just overthinking, as usual. There's no way the mystery girl is going to be in our group. No way the universe is cruel enough to put me through that.

Our group is tucked in the back corner of the class, so most of the stragglers have found their groups. There's only one person left looking for a group now, and it's the mystery girl. She glances over at us, realizing that we're the only group she hasn't checked with yet, and she makes her way towards us. We locked eyes from across the class, her honey brown eyes as breathtaking as I remember. Finally she reaches us.

"Hey, I'm Fiona. Are you Jack?" she asks.

She directs the question at me, and I stare back at her, momentarily too stunned to speak. This girl, who I've been fantasizing about for months, who I've tried to talk to and even sat beside, is standing right in front of me. Talking to me. Sure she doesn't know my name yet, but that's besides the point.

"I'm Roman actually. That's Jack," I say, gesturing blindly to one of the other guys in our group.

"Actually, I'm Aaron, that's Jack," says Aaron.

Normally I'd be embarrassed that I got someone's name wrong to their face, but at that moment, I can't focus on anyone except the mystery girl. Or I guess I should say, Fiona.

The rest of the class goes by in a haze. Not like the depressive, non feeling haze I'd been experiencing for the past few weeks, but more of a dream-like haze. Where you can't believe this is real life. The professor could've been telling us the secret to magically acquiring a million dollars, and I would've never known.

The end of class comes, and Fiona stops us to exchange phone numbers, and set up a meeting time at the library. Aaron and Jack seem less than enthusiastic about it, but I figured this was a perfect opportunity for me to talk to Fiona. If you had told me a few months ago that I'd be hanging out with her outside of a class setting, and somehow got her phone number, I would've jumped for joy.

As usual, the library is packed. I'm the first one there, and I luck out and find a table tucked away in the corner on the first floor, near the cafe. The smell of coffee beans in the air helps calm my nerves a little bit.

"Hey. Roman, right?"

I look up, startled to find a pair of glimmering honey brown eyes looking back at me. Fiona manages to find my spot without texting first to ask where we were meeting.

"You're here early. I assumed I'd be the first one to get here. I was walking around looking for a place to sit, and saw you," says Fiona as she sits down in the seat across from me.

"Yeah, I'm just that dedicated to the project."

I actually got to the library an hour earlier than our meeting time. After my internship, instead of going to the gym, I spent an hour and a half trying to decide what I should wear, and then decided I should get here early so I'm not embarrassingly sweaty like I'd normally be. I picked a table that's off to the side, out of the way so I'd be more comfortable and feel more in control of the situation, but all of my prep is rendered useless once I lay eyes on Fiona. My heart is beating annoyingly fast, and it feels as if the temperature has gone up ten degrees.

"I would've been here earlier, but some asshole cut me off, and I had to pull over to calm myself down," says Fiona. "My therapist says I need to focus on things I can control, but it's hard not being upset at people like that. The ones with no regard for anyone around them, who probably voted for Trump, and are leading the world to a swift demise."

Fiona's voice is soft, but forceful, her fiery passion seeps into her words, and engrosses me in a way that almost feels like a magic spell has been cast.

"This country is run by arrogant, narcissistic pricks who only care about making more money for themselves. Big Pharma is at the center of it all. Our healthcare system is fucked and the food we're given just makes things worse. We're all doomed you know," says Fiona as she starts to unpack her bag.

All I can do is nod along and try to think of a response that seems smart. Her intensity catches me off guard, but it also puts me at ease, I'm drawn in like a magnet. It feels like the two of us are alone together in our own little bubble. I'm hanging on to her every word, I feel as if I'm in the crowd at a Martin Luther King Jr. speech. I find myself wanting to impress her, but not in the way that I normally would. Usually I shrink from the spotlight, but I want Fiona to see me, I want her to look at me and think that I'm knowledgeable enough to converse with her on this level, and that I value what she has to say too. I find myself craving her attention and respect in a way that I've never felt before.

"I definitely feel as though a lot of our society is built to enslave us into the system. Not even just in the health care system, we have to willingly put ourselves into debt with student loans to be able to get a decent job, we have to put ourselves into even more debt with car notes to be able to get places, and we have to get credit cards to be able to apply for housing, which is something that's a basic human need. You're right when you say we're doomed," I say. My comment isn't exactly Nobel Prize worthy, but

I'm pleased with myself for not just responding with noncoherent gibberish.

"Exactly. There's no reason that America should be so far from other countries in that regard," says Fiona.

"Where would you want to live if you had a choice?" I ask.

"Hmmm I don't know, maybe somewhere in Italy or Egypt. What about you?"

"I think it'd be cool to live in Tokyo. It scares me to live in a country where I don't know the language, but I've always wanted to learn Japanese." Truthfully I've never thought about where I'd want to live outside of America before this conversation. I've never even visited anywhere outside of America. I'm not exactly the explorative type, but talking with Fiona seems to bring it out of me. Even though I'd never really considered it before, the idea to learn Japanese and move to Japan seems like something I've always wanted, but never acknowledged before now.

I spend the next thirty minutes or so working on homework for other classes, and trying to think of things to say to Fiona. Aaron and Jack still haven't shown up, and they haven't said anything in the groupchat that we set up at the end of class.

"Ugh, do you think they're going to show up?" asks Fiona.

"I doubt it. They're mad late now, and they haven't said anything."

Fiona puts her head in her hands. "I really need to do well on this."

I wonder to myself why she feels so pressured to do well. Obviously as a college student you feel pressure in every class to do well. There's too much money on the line, not to mention your future. But she seems to have even more riding on this than a normal student would. Naturally I feel obligated to do whatever possible to make sure this goes well for her.

"Did you have any ideas for what you wanted to do for the project?" I ask. "I was thinking something relationship related.

Like maybe looking at the romantic success of introverts versus extroverts."

"Yeah, that could work. I wish the other guys were here so we could talk it through with them, but I guess they'll just have to be cool with this," she says with a shrug.

Not only have I managed to not break out in a nervous sweat, I actually suggested something that Fiona likes? This must be how LeBron James felt at the end of the series against the Thunder when he won his first ring.

"Yeah, hopefully they actually chip in on this project. It seems like it's going to be too much for just two people," I say, trying to play off how ecstatic I feel inside.

"Okay, so this is off topic, but are you the guy that came up to me on the last day of spring semester and told me to have a good summer?"

The optimism I felt a second earlier rapidly evaporates. I feel my cheeks start to redden, well, metaphorically speaking they redden. The blushing process for black people is more of a feeling than a perceptible occurrence. My face and neck burn so viciously that I'm reminded of those Youtube videos of people baking cookies on cars during hot summer days. I imagine if there was cookie dough around, it would burn instantly once it came in contact with my skin. The pores on my skin begin to open like a present on Christmas morning. The nervous sweat that I was so proud of repressing, refusing to be held back any longer.

I don't know why I assumed that I could get through this without her bringing up that embarrassing moment. I cringe internally thinking back on how I stuttered over my words, barely able to make eye contact. Maybe I should try to pretend that wasn't me. Or, maybe I should pretend it was a bet or something. College guys do weird stuff like that all the time. But there's a certain level of lucidity that I see when I look in her eyes. Like no matter what lie I try to sell, she'll see right through it.

"Yeah, that was me," I say as I look down at the table. Not knowing what else to say to make me seem like less of a weird loser.

"This is going to sound silly, but that really helped me. My ex and I had just broken up, and that day I got the dates mixed up on one of my finals and missed it. So I failed the class. That's the reason I really need to do well in this class," says Fiona. "Anyway, the...absurdity of the situation helped snap me out of the mood I was in. So I wanted to thank you," Fiona says, flashing me one of the most brilliant smiles I've ever seen.

I...helped her? I recall her red, puffy eyes, and the wistful expression on her face. The most awkward, cringe worthy moment of my life, the thing that haunted me for months, and she looks back on it fondly. I can't help but laugh.

"Well if you need any more awkward situations to make you feel better, I'm your guy."

Fiona laughs, a soft laugh that sounds better than any song I could ever imagine. "I'll keep that in mind. Well, I guess the others aren't coming, so I have to head out. I'll see you in class."

As she gets up and grabs her stuff to leave, I briefly consider walking out with her. Maybe I'll even have the guts to ask her on a date. But no, I can tell I'm still not ready for that. Her thanking me for my social ineptitude is hardly a license to ask someone on a date. Still, the fact that I was able to help her at all fills me with a sense of pride and self satisfaction that I haven't felt in a long time. It's probably better if I let things end for the night like this instead of risking my luck any further.

I've never had a more stimulating conversation than the one that I had with Fiona tonight. I feel the same way I do after finishing a tough workout, it's almost like an adrenaline rush. For the first time in several weeks, I feel the fog around me start to lift.

THE TAILGATE

The campus always looks so beautiful during the fall. The leaves change to brilliant shades of orange, maroon, and red. I'm reminded of a scene from *When Harry Met Sally*, when the two main characters are walking in a park with the colorful leaves in the background. Walking around campus makes me feel as if I'm walking around in my own movie too. The air slowly becomes more crisp and chilly as the days pass. The summer heat that at one point seemed to be unrelenting, finally starts to dwindle.

This is my favorite time of year. We've finally made it past Halloween, and Thanksgiving's just around the corner, and then Christmas after that. This year for Halloween, like every other year since we've gotten to college, Tristan and I had gone to a costume party. It was my first outing since the incident with Dalton and Olivia. I let Tristan convince me to go out because—well, I don't really know why, I guess being around Fiona every day is having a positive effect on my mental well being. Every year, I try to find creative ways to technically be in a costume without having to dress up. This year, I went as an early voter. I wore my regular clothing with the addition of an early voter sticker. Tristan went as Tarzan, which I think he just wanted to use as an excuse to be shirtless in public. It was a pretty uneventful night, there were no cops or anything, which I was thankful for. I was especially thankful for the fact that I didn't run into Olivia. That would've been super awkward, and I wasn't prepared for those memories to be brought back up.

I did think it was interesting, however, that Tristan hasn't been bringing anyone back to our dorm as often as he did last year. Last Halloween, I had to drive Tristan and some drunk girl back to our dorm, and the year before that, Tristan went home with some girl he met. This year he didn't go home with anyone, and he barely even went out of his way to flirt with anyone the way he normally would. I wonder if whatever happened with him and Liz has gotten to him. I can only imagine how it must feel to be disappointed by something like this that he waited so long for.

Later today, we're going to the tailgate together so maybe he'll be more himself then. It's my first tailgate of the season. My social battery is fully charged, and I feel like this is a good opportunity for a fresh start on my social life, which had taken a hit while I was busy hibernating. Maybe it'll be good for Tristan too.

Right now though, I'm sitting outside on one of the benches by the fountain in the quad area, working on my graphic novel. I have another month before I have to submit it into the competition. The last competition I participated in, back in September, I ended up finishing in seventeenth place. I was kind of bummed out about it because only the top five participants are the ones that get cash prizes, all the other participants get is the experience. Getting seventeenth place out of a pool of close to two hundred people is encouraging though.

My graphic novel is meant to be about this guy who accidentally kills the most popular superhero in the world and becomes depressed. He becomes an assassin, trying to redeem himself by killing bad people. The comic I'm submitting into the competition is a chapter from that graphic novel.

The main character is an outcast, like me. There's a lot of myself in the character, I guess that's why I feel so attached to the story. That, and me wanting to finally have some kind of recognizable achievement. I often fantasize about how good it'll feel to be able to hold my own graphic novel and show it to others as a way of showing my skill and hard work.

There's just one problem, I can't draw all that well. The story part is easy, but drawing something that's good enough for me to win the competition is the hard part. It's probably why I didn't make it into the top five of the last competition. I've been practicing and watching tutorials, but my drawing skills still aren't up to par.

The only positive part of the last month and a half of mild depression is the fact that I've had a lot of time to work on my comic. I've had more time to practice, more time to craft my story and flesh out the characters. I always seem to write better when I'm in a mood. Especially a story like this where the main character is battling his own mental demons, it's like I can funnel some of my own issues into the character. Who needs therapy when you can transfer all of your problems onto a fictional character.

Speaking of my minor psychological problems, I haven't had any of the random pangs of sadness that I'd been having for a while, but the feeling of nothingness still persists. The only exception is in my social psychology class with Fiona. It's as if Fiona is a colorful rainbow across the dull gray sky that represents every other aspect of my life. We've sat next to each other every day since the meeting at the library, which was two and a half weeks ago. My nerves still haven't lessened, any time she's around me the butterflies are out of control. The two other guys in our group haven't really contributed anything so far, so I think

I'm her favorite right now. Maybe if we do well enough on the project I'll work up the courage to properly ask her out.

The way I feel about Fiona makes me feel alive, and hopeful. It's a nice feeling, but in my experience, there's nothing more dangerous than hope. Everytime I feel hopeful about a girl I end up getting hurt in the end. Badly. And as much as I liked Jade, and Olivia, I can tell that I'm going to like Fiona even more. Which means my inevitable failure will lead to an unprecedented amount of hurt. And the thing about hope is despite the fact that I know the hurt and the pain will almost certainly come, there's always that small sliver of optimism. There may be a 99% chance of failure, but maybe just maybe that 1% will pay off, and instead of unprecedented hurt, I'll be able to experience unprecedented happiness. Maybe for once things will work out for me. Through all the heartache, that belief is what keeps me going, but it's a blessing and a curse. That belief is also what makes the heartache so much worse.

The holiday season means it's time to buy gifts for people. One of my talents in life is giving gifts, and now that Camryn has come into my life, I have to get her a gift too. I'm conflicted about what kind of gift to get her though, because while we're friends, I'm starting to feel like maybe we can be more. We've been spending a lot of time together, and it's becoming harder and harder to resist the urge to try to push things further. This is why I haven't ever been able to be friends with a woman who's single. Once these thoughts start creeping into my head, it's like a disease that slowly corrupts my brain. It becomes like an itch that I can't stop from scratching. Before, she had a man, and I was talking to Jade. Then there was Olivia, but Camryn and her man broke up. Now we're both just single. I think back to Tristan telling me how good she has been for me, how cool she is, and obviously she's pretty. So maybe I should just go for it.

I've had the idea of being with Fiona in my head for a while, but in some ways it seems like I think of Fiona as almost like a celebrity crush. Being with her seems as far fetched as me saying I want to be with Zendaya. Ultimately I guess it's kind of ridiculous that I'm sitting here trying to decide between two amazing girls when I probably can't get with either of them.

Since we've been in college, Tristan has started the habit of inviting people I don't really know or like, to the different functions that we go to. Today, however, it's just Tristan, Camryn, and I going together to the tailgate, thankfully. My two closest friends, the two people I trust the most. As someone that's more extroverted, I feel like Tristan is born to be the center of a big group, the life of the party if you will. Me on the other hand, I'm definitely most comfortable going out in small, intimate groups.

It's a nice day. The colorful leaves, and blue sky create a beautiful backdrop for the chaos unfolding in the tailgate. It's a little warm, but far from the unbearable heat that plagues the tailgates that take place earlier in the season. There's a nice, crisp breeze in the November air.

"You want a beer?" Tristan asks Camryn, as he does the thing where he magically produces two beers from thin air.

"Sure, I'll take one," says Camryn.

The tailgate as usual is completely swamped with people. There are several tents set up, and each individual tent has its own music blaring with people dancing in them. Walking around trying to avoid people while all of the sound converges on you from all angles is even more disorienting than it sounds. As we walk around, trying to decide which tent to go into first, Tristan is greeted by the usual wave of attention that he garners any time he goes out to a party or social gathering, by random people I've never seen before. I'm surprised to see Camryn get greeted by a number of people too. It's impressive how quickly she's acclimated to a new school. Seeing her surrounded by people she knows, and already befriended, she looks like she's completely at ease, in her element. I'm standing a few feet away, but her smile radiates a certain joy that I can feel even from where I'm standing. She's never looked prettier to me.

As I'm waiting off to the side, watching Tristan and Camryn be social butterflies, I hear a voice from behind me. "Well look who it is. Is that a ghost I see?"

I turn around to see Dante and Wayne, two guys I know from my comic book club. Or I guess I should say, "knew", past tense. I haven't been to any of the meetings since late september, when the thing with Olivia happened and I was too embarrassed and depressed to go anywhere.

"Hey guys," I say awkwardly.

"Hey, Roman. Where have you been the past couple months?" Dante asks.
"Oh, you know, a little of this, a little of that."

"Well we miss you in the club, how is your comic coming?"

"I'm putting the finishing touches on it. I'm going to submit it for the Stan Lee comic contest at the end of the month."

"Good luck. Make sure you let us see it when it's done," says Wayne. "Also, we want you to know that you're always welcome to come back to the club."

As they walk away, I feel my spirits lift. The feeling of being seen and accepted is new to me. Usually when I go out with Tristan somewhere, I'm an afterthought, I might as well be invisible. It's nice being acknowledged for once. It feels good to have a small group of my own outside of Tristan, even if it's just exchanging comic book ideas.

After a few more minutes of walking around, we find a table with cups set up for cup pong. Which is just beer pong, except the cups are filled with water instead of beer.

"You trying to get whooped up on right quick?" Tristan asks me with a grin. "Camryn can be the ref."

Tristan, being a basketball player has a natural advantage when it comes to cup pong, because it requires a similar shooting touch. I've played him countless times, and lost countless times. Even though he has been drinking today and is already starting to pass the "buzzed" phase and is heading towards full on drunk territory, I still don't like my chances. When Tristan is drinking, it's like his hand eye coordination is heightened instead of lessened. At least when it comes to throwing small ping pong balls into plastic cups. I don't want to lose to him again today, in the middle of all these people walking around, with Camryn watching, but what choice do I have? I don't want to look like a chicken.

For fifteen minutes, we play. Three straight games, three straight losses. Camryn tries to offer words of encouragement, but nothing helps. I should've known this would happen, it's not just cup pong, I can't remember the last time I've beaten Tristan in any sort of competition. I'm ready to pack it up and take my L when I hear a familiar voice.

"You do know you're supposed to get the ball in the cups right?"

The curly, dark hair, the soft timbre of her voice, the weirdly overwhelming scent of her vanilla and cinnamon perfume, and those honey brown eyes that seem to be sparkling in the sunlight. It's Fiona. As she gets closer, her aura, her mere presence dazzles me and shakes me to my core. I have to remind myself to breathe.

"Yeah, well, it's harder than it looks."

"Who is this?" Camryn asks with a somewhat bemused look on her face.

"Wait wait, is that–"

"This is Fiona," I say, cutting off Tristan before he can say something embarrassing. "She's in my social psych class."

"Yeah, I'm trying to carry Roman over here to an A on our group project," says Fiona. She flashes a grin that's half the potency of her normal smile, but still enough to momentarily stun me.

"Since you're over here, how about we get a two on two game going?" Tristan says. "I've been handing Roman L's already, now you can lose together. You can call it a team bonding experience."

Part of me wants to say no. Part of me is mortified that Fiona is over here at all, after all, almost literally every girl I've ever liked, who's also known Tristan, has fallen for him instead of me. Maybe Fiona will be charmed by Tristan's cup pong skills. It's already too late for Camryn, she's been hanging around Tristan and I for too long now, but maybe if I say no to this game, there's still hope for me and Fiona. Plus there's the fact that I always lose to Tristan...always. It was bad enough with just Camryn over here, now Fiona has to see me lose too?

The game starts even worse than the previous three did. Camryn's actually pretty good, and I can't hit anything. Fiona's presence is throwing me off my game. Which is saying something considering I'm not that good to begin with. I feel this intense pressure, similar to how it feels when you're standing too close to the edge of a tall cliff. After three rounds, Camryn and Tristan have already taken half of their cups off the board. Fiona and I on the other hand, we've only hit one shot, and Fiona is the one that made it.

Another round goes by, Fiona and Camryn each hit a shot. The next round, Fiona and Tristan hit a shot. Now we have seven more cups to make while Tristan and Camryn only have three. Tristan, Camryn, and Fiona all miss, it's my turn again. Tristan and Camryn both have a decent amount of alcohol in their system by this point, and they're catcalling me, talking trash, laughing. It's all good natured, I know they don't mean to hurt me or anything like that, but I can't help but feel frustrated.

Why is it so hard for me to just do simple things? I couldn't talk to Fiona back in May. I couldn't maintain a relationship with Jade or Olivia. I can't put this stupid ball in the stupid cup right now. I think about bowling with Jade, how good it felt to get those strikes, and how crushing it felt to lose the game, and then lose her a few months later. I think about how close I came to beating Tristan in mini golf with Olivia, and how terrible I felt the next week when I saw Olivia with Dalton. All of these emotions are swirling around inside me. Every time I feel like I'm making progress, I get brought back to Earth. Why should it be any different now?

But then I look over at Fiona. A few weeks ago I was too depressed to leave my room, too ashamed to show my face anywhere, but I'm here now. I made it through that and I'm here with my two closest friends, and Fiona, who a few months ago, I was too scared to even talk to. I guess that's real progress. Progress doesn't always have to be some grand moment, with fireworks and a parade. Sometimes it sneaks up on you in the dark. The tree branch that for years you're able to walk below with no problem, until one day you hit your head on it, and you realize you've grown. Maybe this moment is my tree branch.

Suddenly my body feels tingly. It's as if the pressure that was radiating off of Fiona a second ago has combined with my body, turning into electricity that's flowing through me, giving me strength, like Thor when he's fighting The Hulk and finally learns how to use his powers without his hammer. I'm reminded of the adrenaline rush a few months ago when I was so angry at Dalton and Olivia, except this feels almost peaceful. Instead of feeling out of control, I feel calm, like I've tapped into some hidden part of myself that was sitting behind a locked door, waiting to be unleashed. It's kind of how I felt briefly while I was bowling against Tristan. Suddenly all of the music that was blaring obnoxiously loud, I can't even hear. The cups that looked tiny, and far away look like they're huge, and right in front of me. Like I couldn't miss even if I tried. I take my shot, and hear the satisfying splash of the ping pong ball hitting the water.

The next two rounds, Tristan and Camryn's team hit one shot, and I hit both of my shots. Which means my turn gets extended until I miss. We have four more cups to make if we want to win, Tristan and Camryn are down to their last two. I take my shot and make it. I take another shot, and make that too. Two left now. I take another shot, and make it. Just one more to win. My first win over Tristan in God knows how long. With Camryn and Fiona both watching. The old me would have choked, but I feel different now.

"Don't worry, Roman can't close the deal," says Tristan jokingly.

His words cause me to hesitate just slightly. In that split second, I catch a glimpse of someone with fiery red hair approaching us. It's Olivia, with a couple of her suitemates who I've met a couple of times.

"Hey guys," says Olivia with a smile.

Tristan shoots me a cautious look, before responding. "What's up, Olivia."

After the punch, Tristan's basketball coaches made him and Dalton sit and talk out their issues. From what Tristan has told me, they're not on great terms, but they're teammates, so it's unrealistic for me to expect them to have beef because of me forever. That being said, I doubt I'll ever forgive Dalton, so I was pleased to hear that things with him and Olivia didn't work out.

Olivia turns her attention to me. "Hey, Roman. It's good to see you, you look good."

"Yeah, thanks," I say.

The tension in the air is so thick that you could cut it with a knife. For a few moments Olivia and I stand there staring at each other awkwardly, both of us unsure of what to say next.

"Well, I'll see you around. It's good seeing you," she says again, with another smile as her and her suitemates walk away.

For the past month and a half, I had been fantasizing about that moment. What would it be like seeing Olivia again? Maybe she would beg for me to take her back. Maybe I would beg her to take me back. Maybe I'd take the chance to tell her how upset and hurt I was over what she did. Instead I did none of those things. The anger towards her is gone. The longing I felt for her for so long is gone too. I feel free of her, finally.

I turn back towards the last cup, and without skipping a beat, I shoot the ping pong ball and hear the sweetest splash I've ever heard. Signaling that I made the shot, and ended the game. Inside I'm jumping for joy, like I just won the Super Bowl. I've finally beaten Tristan! I'm officially over Olivia! I try to maintain my composure as well as I can, but I can't hide the smile on my face.

"Well guys, that was fun, but I think I have to get back to my friends now," says Fiona as she turns towards a short light skin girl, who's arguing with a guy who looks like he could be on the cover of a magazine titled *Preppy Frat Boy Monthly*.

"I'll see you in class," I say, giving her a slight wave, still amazed by the game we just played.

It feels good knowing I'm finally making progress.

THE FRIENDSGIVING

It's the Monday after the tailgate, and I'm in my social psych class, attempting to pay attention to the professor while Fiona sits next to me. It's crazy how easily Fiona commands my attention while putting forth very little effort, although even if she wasn't the one sitting next to me, my mind would still continue to wander to the events that transpired Saturday. I can't imagine that day going any better than it did. Usually when I go out, the best I can hope for is to enjoy myself vicariously through Tristan, but this time the good things actually happened to me.

Later that day, after the tailgate, I got a notification saying that Olivia started following me on Instagram again. On Saturday, I felt so much closure. I felt sure that she was firmly in my past. When I saw the notification I didn't feel the urge to talk to her and make up for lost time, I felt more like I was stuck in a never ending time loop. I'm having enough trouble choosing between Camryn and Fiona, I don't need a third person thrown into the mix. But at the same time, I don't know if I'll be able to maintain the same level of restraint if Olivia were to DM me, I am still just a man after all.

I've spent most of this class period trying to make a power ranking of the three girls in my head. I really liked Olivia at one point, but those feelings have burned to ash and scattered into the wind it seems. Unlike the other two girls though, I'm pretty sure she has feelings for me, which counts for a lot. Camryn is cool, and has become my best friend outside of Tristan, but asking her out is a risk. If she says no the friendship is basically over. I can't see how I could remain friends with someone who's rejected me. And then there's Fiona. I still don't know her as well as the other two girls, but I've built her up to be the perfect woman in my head. That being said, she seems to be the least realistic option, considering she's way out of my league.

The professor ends the class and as I'm walking out of the class, back to my dorm, Fiona catches up to me.

"So I have a super weird favor to ask you. All of my friends are busy right now, or I'd ask one of them, but do you have time to go with me to Wal-Mart?"

Of all the stores in the area, Wal-Mart has the best deals, but it's also positioned in a part of town that's known for being sketchy. The last time I went there, I saw someone get arrested in the parking lot, and that sort of thing is the norm there.

"Yeah, I'll go with you. I have the day off from my internship, and I just have to be back in time for this Friendsgiving thing later."

Every year in November, Tristan and I get together for our own mini Friendsgiving. It usually just consists of us getting together and eating random things we bought from the store, but it's a tradition, and I enjoy it. This year, Camryn is joining us which should be cool. I've become really fond of our group over the past few months.

"Thank you, I owe you one," says Fiona.

The truth is that even if I had other plans today, I would happily cancel them if I knew it meant that I got to spend time with Fiona. We see each other almost every day now and it's still not enough. I feel like an addict who needs more and more of their drug of choice to maintain their high. Except in this case, the drug is Fiona, the girl I know I have no chance with. I know my time with her is limited, it's already November, the semester's almost over, I have to make the best out of what I'm given.

In the car, on the way to the store, I can hardly believe what's going on. This girl was such a mystery to me for so long, and now here I am in her car, doing something as rudimentary as going to the store. The song "Yosemite" by Travis Scott and Gunna plays in the car. She tells me it's her favorite song on the album. I think about how Olivia told me she hadn't even listened to Astroworld on our first date. Now Fiona and I have a full conversation breaking down the album, and I didn't start hyperventilating at all. A proud moment for me, if I do say so myself.

"It's a good thing you have a big strong guy like me here to protect you," I say as I look out the window. There are two guys getting into a heated argument in the parking lot.

"Oh, whatever," says Fiona, rolling her eyes with a faint hint of a smile on her face. "Okay, so we're looking for a plastic drawer set. I need something to hold my art supplies."

"I didn't know you were an artist," I say.

This fact seems to make her seem even cooler to me. I can picture her in Paris, painting the Eiffel Tower while eating a baguette. People who can create art are almost like superheroes to me. The ability to create something from nothing is a gift.

"Yeah, I've been drawing, and making paintings since I was in elementary school. It's always been a hobby of mine, but I chose to major in psychology because I find it to be interesting. And I want to have something that I enjoy doing just for myself, without any monetary incentive."

I think of my own hobbies that I have. I wouldn't want my trips to the gym to be ruined by capitalism. Even my comic book writing is mainly driven by the enjoyment I get from putting the stories together, and the desire to be better at it. I completely understand what she means when she says she wants to keep her hobbies to herself. Once money gets involved, it has a habit of ruining everything. Of course someone like Fiona would have such a wise life outlook. But I'm sure someone as cool as her has no interest in hearing about something as dorky as my comic book ideas.

"Yeah I agree with that. I think there's something beautiful about the human condition. Psychology is the best way to learn about it," I say. "I'd like to see some of your work sometime though."

"We'll see, I tend to be a little overprotective of my art, because I don't usually handle criticism well."

"Finally, a flaw. I was beginning to think you were too perfect," I say as Fiona rolls her eyes.

"Look, look!" says Fiona excitedly as she hurries over to the baby clothing section. "Aren't these just the cutest things you've ever seen," Fiona says as she holds up a pair of baby sized shoes. As she holds them up, she flashes me the most dazzling smile I've ever seen. I find myself enchanted by her as I watch her lithe frame gracefully maneuvering through the aisles.

"I had no idea you were so into babies," I say as Fiona inspects a baby sized cookie monster onesie.

"Well right now, I'd be terrified to have a baby, but one day I hope to have a family of my own."

Fiona, the cool, beautiful girl, who is unusually transfixed by baby clothing. Who would've guessed.

"So anyway, who was that girl that came over to us while we were playing cup pong on Saturday?" asks Fiona.

"Oh—you know, she was just...nobody."

I know I'm in dangerous territory now. If I have any hope of ever being with Fiona, I don't want her to think I have feelings for Olivia.

"She's pretty. Do you think she's pretty?"

"She's okay," I say with a shrug. Internally I wanted to shout out "she's pretty but she's nothing compared to you!" Then there'd be a string quartet playing in the background and then we'd kiss and be together forever. But of course something like that could only happen in my own head.

"It seemed like she was into you."

"Yeah, you know, I just have that effect on women," I say as Fiona shoots me a skeptical look. "Okay, actually we were sort of dating for a little while. We weren't like an official couple or any-thing though. She ended up having sex with one of the guy's on the basketball team, so that kind of ended things."

"I'm sorry to hear that. My ex cheated on me, so I know what that's like."

The idea that someone could cheat on a girl like Fiona is absurd to me. If we were together I don't think I'd ever even think of another woman.

"Look at us, bonding over shared traumatic experiences."

We're walking back to her car, after Fiona finds the plastic drawer set she was looking for.

"Thanks again for coming with me," says Fiona.

Little does she know that I should be the one thanking her. A few months ago I would've killed to have alone time with her even if it was just a trip to the store. Part of me wishes I could say something like "No problem, you can pay me back by letting me take you on a date." That would be cool. That's what Tristan would say, probably. But I'm not Tristan. Despite the fact that this trip let me see a more human, less perfect side of Fiona, I still find myself to be intimidated by her presence. I've put her on such a high pedestal that I don't know if I'll ever have the guts to ask her out.

I make it back to my dorm with enough time to get ready for the Friendsgiving dinner with Tristan and Camryn. I'm bringing a pecan pie, which is my favorite dessert, and some orange chicken that I picked up from Wal-Mart.

"Ahh pecan pie, typical Roman," says Tristan as he walks in with a box of pizza.

"Look man, the pecan pie hits every time," I say with a shrug.

"Yeah yeah yeah," says Tristan. "What did you get into today?"

I tell Tristan about my trip to the store with Fiona. And about how she brought up Olivia randomly.

"Yeah, that's tough. Definitely gotta be careful in that situation. Olivia was giving off strong flirty vibes with you on Saturday though, so I can't blame Fiona for asking."

"You think so? She followed me on Instagram again, I'm waiting to see if she messages me."

"Man, you can't go back to Olivia, she did you dirty."

"I know, but at least I know she likes me. Or at least I'm pretty sure."

"What about Fiona? I mean going to the store with someone is a pretty intimate activity. When was the last time you went grocery shopping with someone you didn't like?"

"Yeah, but that could just be a friendly platonic thing you know? Plus Fiona's way out of my league, there's no way I could pull that off."

"The only way to make sure someone is out of your league is by telling yourself over and over again that they're out of your league," says Tristan as he cracks open a can of Coke.

"I guess. I don't know, maybe I should just focus all of my energy on Camryn. It seems like the universe is pointing me in that direction. I think I may actually have feelings for her now."

"I—uh I'm not sure if that's the best idea," says Tristan hesitantly.

"Why not? You've been telling me she was right for me this whole time, and now you change your mind?"

Before Tristan can answer, there's a knock on the door, it's Camryn.

"Hey, guys, what's going on?" She's carrying a container with collard greens and another one with yams. "I thought this was supposed to be a Friendsgiving. Why didn't y'all bring any traditional Thanksgiving dishes? Not even Turkey."

"Pecan pie is a Thanksgiving dish," I say with a slight grin.

"And pizza should be a Thanksgiving dish," says Tristan.

"Yeah yeah whatever," says Camryn with a smile. "Thank you guys for inviting me to this, I've never been to a Friendsgiving before."

"You've become one of the gang. We're like the Three Musketeers," I say.

It's really crazy how someone who I didn't know existed at the beginning of the summer, has become such a large, integral part of my life. Fiona is cool, but Camryn is real. We've gotten so close over these last six months, she's impacted my life in a major, positive way. Even though Tristan doesn't think I should go after her anymore, it seems like this is my golden opportunity. My chance to finally experience a real relationship with someone I know cares about me.

"So, Camryn, we were talking about Fiona. Our boy Roman over here thinks she's out of his league."

Camryn rolls her eyes as she takes a bite out of the orange chicken I bought. "Roman, how many times do I have to tell you that you're a good guy? You're handsome, you're charming, and you're cool. Nobody's out of your league."

I feel the blood rush to my face at this statement. I'll never get used to her compliments, but I appreciate them nonetheless.

"Handsome? You sound like somebody's aunt," Tristan says jokingly.

"Oh, shut up, don't be jealous that I'm complimenting Roman and not you. Fiona was cool though. I like her more than I liked Olivia I think. And I'm not just saying that because of what happened with her and DJ."

"Yeah, she was cool, even though y'all found a way to cheat in the cup pong game against us. I don't know how yet, but there's no doubt that there was some foul play going on," says Tristan.

"That's perfect actually. You can tell her that she has to come over for a rematch with us or something. That'll give you an excuse to invite her over, and there will be less pressure because we'll be here with you," says Camryn.

I don't know how I feel about that. The tailgate was one thing, because I didn't invite her, Fiona just saw us playing cup pong and kind of just invited herself. The other times we've hung out, there's been a reason for it, usually the project. Inviting her over just to hang out would bring more expectations, more pressure. It's like a declaration that I'm shooting my shot. I have a feeling that if I did that I would end my chances of becoming more than friends with Camryn too.

"I don't know, I feel like there's a good chance she would decide not to come. I still don't think she likes me like that, and I doubt she would be down for that."

"At least this way you'll know for sure," says Camryn.

The rest of the Friendsgiving goes by smoothly. We turned on the *Charlie Brown Thanksgiving* special, which is one of my favorites, while we finished our bountiful feast, and then talked like old friends. As someone that grew up watching shows like *How I Met Your Mother*, it's nice to have a group of my own.

After the dinner was over and everyone retired to their respective rooms, I'm left to reflect on the day. I got to spend time outside of class, alone, with Fiona which is definitely a good thing, even if she's not into me in the way I'd like. Then there was Friendsgiving and getting to see Camryn. According to Camryn, I'm a charming, handsome guy that anyone would be lucky to be with. Maybe that's her way of telling me that she's interested. Maybe this whole time she's been trying to give me little hints that she might want more too. But then she also pushed me to go after Fiona, and so did Tristan. It feels as if there's a civil war going on in my heart. I've never been so conflicted. I guess I just have to hope that I make the right decision.

THE BLINDSIDE

It's the day after Thanksgiving break, there's a certain energy in the air that only comes around Christmas time. The end of the semester is near, and the students are all limping to the finish line. It's the most difficult, most stressful part of the semester, but I've always enjoyed it. There's Christmas music and movies, and it's right before a three week break. Usually by this point I'm ready for a fresh start, but this semester is different. Before Thanksgiving break, Fiona and I were on good terms. We'd been texting everyday the past few weeks, and meeting up a few times a week to work on the project together. She even texted me saying Happy Thanksgiving, with emojis and everything. I'm worried that after this semester I won't see her again though. Right now, the project is forcing us to spend time together, but once that's over, she really has no incentive. Although I said the same thing about Camryn, and things are still going pretty well with us.

"What are you about to do right now? Do you want to go get lunch at the dining hall?"

It's the end of class, one of the last classes before we start the presentations. Fiona's question lingers in the air like smoke from a fire. We've made it a habit to walk with each other after class until one of us gets to the next building we have to go to. This is different than just walking around campus together though. A sit down, shared dining experience is way more formal. Is Fiona...asking me on a date? No no, surely not. I mean it's just the dining hall. The dining hall isn't exactly a beacon of romance, but still.

"You mean just the two of us? Like alone?" I ask as I feel the heat rise to my face.

Fiona laughs softly. Even though I know it's in a teasing manner, to me it still sounds sweeter than an ice cream sundae. "Is that going to be a problem for you?"

"I just wasn't expecting to be asked on a date today, I'm totally underdressed."

"Oh, relax, it's just lunch. I would ask one of my other friends but they're busy again today, and I'm hungry."

There it is, not a date. It's probably for the best. When I picture our future first date, it's at a nice restaurant, overlooking the ocean, while dolphins are jumping out of the water, and someone is playing the harp in the background. There's another fantasy I have where I rent out a whole stadium and have dinner in the middle of the field, like Drake did, but even I must admit that one's a little far-fetched.

"Speaking of friends of yours, what's the deal with that girl we saw at the tailgate? The one that got into an argument with that guy?"

"Oh yeah, Sam, she's a bit of a hothead. Honestly you're lucky none of my other friends are coming with us today. They'd eat you alive," says Fiona. "I always feel like I have to look after them. I guess I'm the mom of the group."

"I like to think of myself as the uncle of my group. The uncle that's off doing his own thing, that doesn't like responsibility. Don't you ever get tired of having to look after your friends when they get a little too drunk?"

I remember the time that Tristan got way too drunk one night when we were in the city, and he ended up vomiting in the Uber on our way home. My first ever one star review on my otherwise flawless five star résumé. It's hard enough watching out for myself, let alone a whole other person too. That's how I know I'm not yet ready for fatherhood.

"No, I mean, I don't know, I kind of like getting to watch over them. It's a burden of love. There have been a few times when my friends have called me in the middle of the night to pick them up. I guess it's just a part of my nature."

Oh Fiona, beautiful, wise, and nurturing. How could anyone not be smitten by her? Every time she speaks it's like I got hit by another one of cupid's arrows. If only it went both ways.

"Yeah, you really do sound like a mom right now."

"Oh, shut up," Fiona says as she lightly pushes my shoulder.

We get into the dining hall, and it feels different than it usually does. Obviously I've been to the dining hall countless times, but I'm almost always alone, listening to music or a podcast, in my own world. Now, though, being with Fiona it's like I'm out in the open, exposed. It's like I'm in a brand new world that I haven't experienced before. It's uncomfortable for me, feeling people's eyes on us. I find a table that's off to the side, out of the way of all the hustle and bustle.

"So you're a bit of an introvert aren't you," says Fiona as she comes to the table with a plate of spaghetti and garlic bread.

"Uh, what makes you say that?"

"Oh you know, the tables you pick out. This one and whenever we go to the library you pick one that's out of the way. I figure it's either that or you're ashamed to be seen with me," Fiona says with a shrug.

"Why would I be ashamed to be seen with you?"

"I know how you guys are. You probably have some hoes around that you don't want to see you out with another girl."

"Wow you must be a mind reader, that's exactly what I was thinking," I say jokingly. "Yeah no actually, I'm pretty introverted. I think I have social anxiety. I'm nervous about our presentation, they usually don't go well for me."

"My brother's kind of like that too."

"It's a curse. God saw that he made me too awesome, so he gave me crippling social anxiety to balance it out."

"Yeah right, too awesome," says Fiona as she rolls her eyes. "Is that why you were so weird the first time you tried to talk to me?"

I remember how it felt the first time I tried to talk to her. I don't have asthma, but I imagine it's a similar sensation. The crushing feeling in my chest, like all of the air around me, was compressing me down into a little ball. Momentarily forgetting how to speak. The pressure of her presence was so intense it made me long for the uncomfortable presentations I had to give. Now I'm sitting here talking with the same girl that made me feel that way. Life is funny sometimes.

It's cool that we've gotten to a place where we can talk so openly about something as awkward as that moment in the quad, but it's a hard question to answer. Am I supposed to just tell her that I couldn't talk to her like a normal person because within seconds of laying eyes on her, I had already developed a massive crush on her? I'm not beating the "weird guy" allegations with that one. Before I can answer, I see Wayne, one of the guys from the comic book club, walk over to our table.

"Hey, Roman, how are you?"

"What's up Wayne, this is Fiona," I say.

Wayne gives Fiona a polite wave before turning his attention back to me. "I read your graphic novel, it's pretty fire. I left you some comments to consider, I'll email it back to you tonight."

After running into Dante and Wayne at the tailgate, I decided to send them my graphic novel, and the shorter comic version to get their thoughts on it. It makes me nervous sharing my work with people I know, but I figure it's worth it if it makes the graphic novel better. I didn't expect to see him now, when I'm with Fiona though. I'm sure whatever cool points I had mounting up have been vaporized by this revelation that I am writing a graphic novel. Writing a graphic novel has to be like the dorkiest, nerdiest, geekiest thing someone could do. Which is probably why I never felt comfortable enough to tell Jade, Olivia, or Fiona until now. I was afraid of being viewed negatively because of my weird hobby. But I guess there's nothing I can do about it now, the cat's out of the bag.

"Oh, I didn't know you were making a graphic novel," says Fiona with a look of curiosity on her face. "Why didn't you tell me? I told you about my artwork."

Wayne shoots me an apologetic look. "Oh...sorry about that, I didn't know you hadn't let other people know about it yet. I'll hit you up about it later though," he says as he hesitantly walks away.

Fiona's eyes bulge, and she exaggerates covering her mouth, feigning surprise. "Wow, well I gotta say Roman, I'm feeling a little betrayed. How could you not tell me you were trying to make a graphic novel?"

"I don't know, I mean I guess I just didn't think you'd be interested."

"What's it about?"

"Oh it's silly, you don't need to know all the details...You know they really put a lot of effort into these turkey burgers, they taste almost as good as regular hamburgers," I say, trying to change the subject.

"Forget about the turkey burger," Fiona says, as her eyes cut into me like daggers.

"Okay okay. It's about this guy who is ostracized from a young age, and he trains obsessively to win this tournament to prove himself. Well in the finals of the tournament, he accidentally kills his opponent who happens to be this hero who's beloved by everyone. Then the main character becomes an assassin and tries to cope with his loneliness and self loathing. It's semi-inspired by this anime called *One Punch Man.*"

"That sounds really interesting. I like *One Punch Man,* Saitama isn't an assassin though."

"Really I meant in the sense that the character has an existential crisis over how strong he is relative to everyone around him, and he has to learn how to exist in the world."

Fiona watches *One Punch Man* and thinks my graphic novel idea is interesting? I must be dreaming or something. From what I can tell, whenever something goes my way, the universe has a way of countering that with something bad. I'm sure whatever this stroke of good fortune is will soon come to an end.

"But yeah I really like the whole process. It's been therapeutic. The last competition I entered into I got seventeenth place. I just have to work on the artwork, I think I'll do better in the next one."

"You need help with artwork? I can help you with that," says Fiona excitedly.

"I don't know, I think I might be a lost cause, I've tried all kinds of different tutorials."

"But never one of mine," Fiona says as she meticulously plucks the meatballs out of her spaghetti.

"Why are you taking out the meatballs from your spaghetti? That's the best part."

"I'm a vegetarian. Do you know how much water it takes to raise cattle? All the hormones they put in the animals? Not to mention the inhumane treatment of the animals. It's horrible."

I've gotten used to the impassioned, idealistic rants that Fiona goes on. Most times it's about things I've never even considered, so I always find them to be interesting and informative. I've never been around someone so knowledgeable and headstrong, my conversations with her usually leave me feeling invigorated. Plus it makes me feel good knowing that she feels comfortable enough to open up around me in that way. I think she also appreciates that I put in the effort to pay attention to what she's saying. This is the first time that one of her rants is semi aimed in my direction though, I look down at my half eaten turkey burger, with guilt in my heart. I wonder if this is how people feel when I tell them I don't drink alcohol, when they have a drink in their hand. I feel my appetite dwindling.

"Oh don't be so dramatic," says Fiona, as if reading my thoughts...again. "I don't care what you eat, just don't eat pork around me. Pigs are filthy animals."

As we finish up our food, Fiona makes me promise to let her give me drawing lessons. I get to spend more time with her, and I might even help improve my graphic novel. It's a win win.

"Hey, isn't that your friend, Tristan?" Fiona asks, pointing to a poster of Tristan in his basketball uniform as we're leaving the dining hall. "A lot of my friends have a crush on him."

"And what do you think of him?" I ask, as I pretend to scroll through my phone in an attempt to mask my investment in her answer.

"Ehh he's okay, not really my usual type, but he's cool."

Interesting. Tristan is irresistible to most girls, but maybe Fiona's immune.

I feel Fiona's eyes study me for a moment. "You know, you have this calming presence about you. I don't think I've met a guy as chill as you before, it's refreshing."

It's not the first time someone's said something like this to me before, but it's funny to me hearing Fiona say this considering my heart does jumping jacks whenever she's around.

"Well, thank you, my theory is that my natural charisma is so underwhelming that people mistake it for chillness," I say jokingly.

Fiona rolls her eyes. "Anyway, I don't know if I told you this or not, but some of my work is being presented in this art show at the end of the semester."

"Oh really? That's really great," I say enthusiastically.

"Some friends of mine are going, it should be nice. It would mean a lot to me if you went too," says Fiona. With that smile that I couldn't resist even if I wanted to.

"Uh yeah, of course, I'll be there," I say in disbelief.

Fiona, this cool girl who's miles out of my league, is asking me to go to an art show, her art show. That's gotta mean something right? I mean she wouldn't invite just anyone to come see her artwork. And on top of that she said it would "mean a lot to her" if I went. I must be living in a bizarro world or something.

"Okay, cool, well I'll see you in class."

In spite of the long lunch, I somehow manage to make it to my internship on time, and go to the gym afterwards. I finally make it back to my room when I hear a knock on the door. It's Tristan.

"What's up Rome? You trying to go to Harris Teeter right quick?"

Our first couple of years on campus, Tristan and I would always take late night trips to the Harris Teeter close to campus. It was kind of a bonding experience, it's probably why Tristan thought it was a big deal that Fiona asked me to go to the store with her a couple of weeks ago. Now that I have my own car, and Tristan's been so busy with his basketball schedule, we haven't gone on any trips like that all semester, so it's kind of weird that he's asking me now. I guess he must be feeling nostalgic.

"Yeah, okay, let's go."

"So things with you and Fiona, they're...good?" Tristan asks as we comb through the aisles of the Harris Teeter. So far all he's picked up is eggnog.

"Yeah I guess. We got lunch today, and she invited me to her art show."

"That's good, that's what's up," Tristan says with a little more enthusiasm than I would expect to hear.

It's early December now, and the Harris Teeter is decked out in Christmas decoration. One of my favorite things about the holidays is seeing all of the decorations.

"You remember that one Christmas, before my parent's divorce when they were arguing all day and I had to come to your house as an escape?" I ask.

"Yeah, the year it actually snowed on Christmas, and we had a big snowball fight, and I accidentally gave you a nosebleed."

I don't know why that specific memory comes to mind on this random December night. Just another one of the countless times that Tristan has been there for me in my life.

"We gotta get a Christmas tree for our dorm this year," I say as I look at the small plastic trees Harris Teeter has on display. "We can invite Camryn over to help us decorate it, while we have a Christmas movie playing in the background, and make ginger-bread cookies."

"Yeah that would be cool," says Tristan with uncertainty in his voice.

Okay, it's official, Tristan's acting weird. I don't understand what's going on. The fact that he asked me to come with him here in general is a little strange, and the fact that we're in the check-out line and all he has is the eggnog that he picked up when we first got into the store. Plus he's been uncharacteristically stoic, once Camryn's name was brought up.

"Hey Roman, I think we need to talk," says Tristan as we walk out of the store. He's looking at his shoes with a somber tone. It's the complete opposite of his usual facetious demeanor. I can't remember the last time I heard him sound like this.

"Sure, what's up?" I ask nervously.

"So, Camryn and I...Camryn and I have been kind of seeing each other for a couple of months now."

For a moment there's silence as I try to take in what Tristan has just told me. My perception of reality has crumpled around me. I can practically hear it shatter like broken glass.

I clear my throat and look away, unable to bring myself to look at Tristan. "Seeing each other? What do you mean? When did this happen?"

"The night we went to that party, the day we moved in. After we got back, she came by our room looking for you, but you were asleep.So we were talking for a while and things kind of...escalated."

"Escalated?" I ask, my voice sounding smaller and smaller as more time passes.

"Yeah uh we kind of had sex," says Tristan, still looking down at his shoes. "We both felt really bad about it, and we agreed that it wouldn't happen again. And it didn't, at least not for a while. She was still with Justin, and then I had Liz, but then when I found out things were over between her and Justin, things kind of just happened."

The awkward tension, the guilty looks, it all makes sense now. I guess it's ridiculous that it took me so long to see it.

"We didn't want you to know, at least I didn't. It was just a casual fling at first, I knew how you felt about her, and I didn't want my transgressions to keep you from trying to get with her, if that's what you wanted. But over time I've come to realize that I've never felt about anyone the way that I feel about her. I think I'm in love with her, and I couldn't keep it a secret anymore."

"Oh, okay, yeah I understand," I say despondently.

"I'm sorry for keeping this from you, but I really think we have something special."

At this point, I can barely hear Tristan. It's like I'm underwater, and he's on the surface, trying to say something to me.

"I...I think I'm gonna walk home," I say.

"Come on, Rome. Don't be like this."

"No, it's cool, I just need some time to myself I think," I say, my voice sounding as small as a worm, which matches how I feel.

"Okay, well, I'm sorry," says Tristan before getting in his car to leave. "Text me when you make it back."

I feel betrayed. I've been combing through my mental dictionary for a word that accurately describes how I feel, and betrayal seems to be the closest one. The sting I feel is worse than a million stings from a wasp. I don't know why I feel this way, I mean it's not like Camryn and I were dating or anything. But still, I felt like there was something there. Of all the girls Tristan could go for, of course, it's Camryn. And of course Camryn would fall for Tristan, how silly of me to think otherwise.

I really wasted time trying to compare Camryn to Fiona, as if I had a snowball's chance in hell of being with either of them. What girl in her right mind would want to be with me, when Tristan is right there? And now that Fiona has met Tristan, I'm sure she has a massive secret crush on him too. She probably only invited me to her art show so that I'd bring Tristan as a plus one.

More than anything though, I'm overcome with a profound feeling of jealousy and loneliness. My two best friends in the whole world are together now. How am I meant to still hang out with them, seeing them happy together while I have absolutely no one. The universe is cruel.

After several minutes of walking (my emotional turmoil made me underestimate the walk back to campus) I found myself outside of the gym. The hoodie and sweatpants that I wore to the store aren't exactly the best workout attire, but it'll have to do. I'm still sore from my workout earlier today, but I know if I go back to my room now the demons in my brain will keep me up all night, whispering the dark thoughts that I try so hard to suppress. The gym is my safe haven, a place for me to close myself off from the outside world by playing music so loud that I can't hear myself think, and doing exercises that are so rigorous that all I can manage to do is focus on my breathing and my form. It's a perfect way to clear my head.

I'm in the middle of a set of power cleans when, inexplicably, my music cuts off, and my phone starts to ring. My phone never rings, I make sure to have my do not disturb setting turned on at all times, especially when I'm at the gym, especially when my emotions are as jumbled as they are right now. I know for a fact that my do not disturb is turned on now too because I noticed that Camryn and Tristan have both tried calling and texting me and my phone never went off. Back when Olivia had given me the ultimatum I took Camryn off of my favorites list so she couldn't bypass my do not disturb mode anymore. I've been meaning to add her back on it but I'm grateful now that I didn't. I wonder what this could be, I don't think I have anyone else saved under favorites right now. I look at the screen and see that it's Fiona calling. I realize now that when I first got her number, I was so excited that I automatically saved her under favorites in my contacts, the first and only person I've done that for. This is her first time calling me, usually we communicate through text or in person. A part of me feels kind of excited, it's not every day that your crush calls you out of the blue, but I also feel like maybe I shouldn't answer. I can't imagine I'm the best person to talk to right now. If it was anybody else, I would've just let it ring, but it's not anybody else, it's Fiona. I answered the phone.

"Uhh hello?" I say with uncertainty.

"Hey, Roman."

"Yeah, what's up? Everything okay?"

"Yeah I'm just walking back to my car and wanted to call some-one to scare off any kidnappers. I thought a guy's voice would sound more intimidating, which sounds silly now that I'm saying it out loud," says Fiona with a laugh. "What are you doing?"

"At the gym," I say.

"You're at the gym in the middle of the night?"

I try to cover my face so the two other people currently at the gym with me can't see me grinning at my phone like the love-struck doofus that I am. "Look, it's the middle of the afternoon somewhere in the world. Besides, you're the one that's just now walking to their car to go home."

"That's a fair point. Maybe we can go to the gym together sometime, you know, whenever you decide to go before 11 PM."

I try to keep my composure as I respond. "Yeah, that'd be cool, I'm sure you'd get stronger than me in no time." Ugh why would I say something as dumb as that.

Thankfully Fiona seems to find this amusing. "Yeah okay, I'm looking forward to it. Well I'm in my car now, I'll see you in class."

When the call ends I'm dumbfounded. Not only did Fiona ask to go to the gym with me, of all the guys she could've called, she chose to call me, that's got to be a good sign. I'm sure I'm reading too much into things as usual, but it's nice to fantasize, my mind is so distracted by Fiona that I'm temporarily freed from my thoughts regarding Camryn and Tristan. I clean off the bar-bell and go back to my dorm, carried by the dream of Fiona and I going on gym dates together.

THE INNER SANCTUM

It's the last day before our presentation, and my group is putting the finishing touches on our project. It looks like we actually did a good job with it. Jack and Aaron didn't do much, but they did just enough. Now hopefully, I can get them to do most of the talking, that's the real benefit of group projects. As much as I hate presenting, I'm kind of thankful for the project, because it's distracted me from the whole Tristan Camryn situation.

Over the past week, Fiona and I have been spending even more time together. Working on the project and helping each other study for exams. The news that Tristan and Camryn had been sneaking around the past couple of months has made it weird for me to be around them. Okay, maybe I haven't actually tried to be around them yet, but it's kind of hard to willingly put yourself in a position to be around your two closest friends, when they're together. Especially considering I had feelings for one of them. I've been actively avoiding them all week. With Tristan, it's easy, the basketball season is in full swing, so even if things were normal I'd be lucky to see him once over the course of a week. Camryn on the other hand, has been a little more difficult. Once she found out that Tristan and I talked, and that I didn't take it as positively as one may have hoped, she's been texting me, apologizing, wanting to meet up. She even offered to take me to Sonic, and pay for my food like I did for her after her breakup with Justin. But the thought of seeing her is just too much for me right now. I've told her I just need some space, but she just took that as a sign to try harder. At least it's almost the end of the semester. It'll be easier to avoid them once I'm back home.

"I can go first, Jack you go after me, then Roman, then Aaron can close it out," says Fiona.

"I'm cool with that," I say.

Honestly as long as I'm not first or last, those are the two spots that have the most pressure. I mean having to speak at all is going to suck, but at least I won't have that added pressure.

"Okay, cool is that all?" Aaron asks, as he checks his phone. "Jack and I are supposed to be meeting some people at a bar to watch the Packers vs. Bears game tonight."

The NFL has Thursday night games, but most of them are trash. The game tonight, is one of the first actual good ones all season, so I understand Aaron's rush to leave.

"Okay, just make sure you guys are ready for tomorrow," says Fiona.

Fiona and I walk out of the library together.

"Since we're apparently pairing up now, what are you about to get into?" I ask, not expecting her to actually invite me to do anything.

"Uhh nothing actually. What about you? Are you going to a bar to get drunk and watch that silly little football game too?"

"Who me? I don't even like football," I say sarcastically. I've actually been waiting all day to get home to watch this game. I might even order a pizza.

Fiona laughs. "Now I know that's a lie. I see you wearing football stuff all the time."

"Well either way, I'm not going to a bar. Kind of an overrated experience for someone who doesn't drink," I say with a shrug.

"Oh, you don't drink? Why not?"

I briefly considered telling her about my cousin, and how we got into an accident because of a drunk driver, but I decided not to. The last thing I want is to see that look of pity on Fiona's face.

"Oh, you know, it just doesn't seem like it was for me. I'd probably just send a bunch of emotional texts to people."

"Well I think it's cool. It makes you unique," says Fiona.

"I appreciate you not trying to convince me into it. Most people tell me that I should try it at least once before I die."

"Those people are dumb, they just want to bring you down to their level."

We make it to Fiona's dorm. I watch Fiona walk towards the front door, and I'm about to leave, when she stops and turns around.

"Do you want to come up? You can practice your drawing."

I'm at a loss for words. Fiona's really inviting me upstairs...where her room is? That's where people have sex, but even without sex, seeing where someone lives and sleeps is an extremely intimate thing. Tristan and Camryn are the only people that have seen my room.

What if her roommates are there? It'd be mad awkward for them to see me walk in with Fiona. Unless she has guys over often. Then I guess this would just be another Thursday for her. Ugh I don't want to think about that.

What if her roommates aren't there? It'd just be the two of us in there...alone. Anything could happen at that point. I think back to the time Olivia asked me to come up to her room. I was beyond nervous, and couldn't go through with it. Now though, despite my nerves, and the game I'd have to miss by deciding to go with her, I kind of want to go. It's like a forbidden, behind the scenes look at Fiona that I'd never get to see otherwise. The more time I can spend with her, the better.

"Yeah, okay, sure. The game can wait."

We get into her dorm, and there's a short, light skin girl sitting on the couch on her computer. It's the girl I saw at the tailgate, I think Fiona said her name is Sam.

"Hey, Fiona, who's this?" asks Sam.

"This is Roman, the boy from my social psych class."

Sam gives me a look like she's trying to examine my worthiness. "Ahh, so this is Roman. Fiona's told me a lot about you."

Fiona's told her friends about me? That's gotta be a good thing right? At least it seems that way, the way Sam is acting.

"I'm just glad she's a part of my group," I say with a sheepish grin.

"Oh you mean so she can do all the work and you can sit back and do nothing?"

"N-no I just meant-"

"Do you go to the dorm of every girl you work on projects with?"

"Only the ones with cool roommates, like you," I manage to squeak out.

"Uh-huh, well just make sure you guys don't do anything too crazy once you get in her room."

Fiona's cheeks redden. "Stop Sam, I'm just helping him with his drawing."

"Yeah, okay," says Sam with a wink.

Fiona's room is not what I was expecting. For one thing, there were a bunch of coverings over what looked to be canvas shaped objects. She also has a ton of candles everywhere. At least twenty, maybe thirty. There are also a variety of different lotions and perfume bottles. It looks like the inside of a Bath and Body Works store.

Fiona hands me a drawing pad. "Here, you can draw on this."

"Where should I sit?" I ask. There's only one chair in the room, and it looks like Fiona's going to be using it to sit at her desk.

"You can sit on the bed."

"O-on the bed?" I ask hesitantly.

Fiona laughs. "Oh come on don't make it weird."

I oblige, and hop on the bed. She usually gives me different drawing prompts to practice drawing. She'll draw it first, so I can see her process, and then I'm supposed to copy it until it looks somewhat passable.

"So what's with all the coverings? Am I not worthy of seeing your art?" I ask as I try to draw Spider-Man climbing up a wall.

"You just have to wait until the art show. I'm trying to incentivize you."

"Ahh come on, you know I'm gonna be there regardless."

"Okay, so then you should have no problem with waiting until then."

Dammit her logic is as flawless as her impeccable smile.

"Ugh, this is so annoying," says Fiona, looking down at her phone.

"What's wrong?

"My mom's been bugging me all day. My parents aren't on good terms. They refuse to get a divorce, but it's clear that they hate each other. My mom's been venting to me all day about something my dad did."

"That sucks, I'm sorry to hear that. My parents got divorced when I was younger. I'm thankful for it everyday."

"Yeah, it just sucks, like I tell them both that they need to see a therapist to talk about their issues but they don't listen. One of the reasons I wanted to major in psychology was so that I can help couples like my parents."

"Do you ever worry that your parents might have rubbed off on you in a bad way? I worry that I might have picked up some of their dysfunctional traits and that when I meet someone I really like I'll ruin it."

"I've felt that way too. I feel like majoring in psychology makes you more aware of your problems but doesn't tell you how to fix them."

"I guess we just have to hope that when we find the right person, we'll be able to work through it," I say.

I desperately want to tell Fiona that I'm the right person for her and that we can work out our issues together, but I'm sure I'd just freak her out. Plus I'm sure I have way more issues than her. I can't imagine hurting Fiona though, even with whatever issues I may have, I think I'd get it together if I was with her.

"Fiona, when I told you that the reason I didn't drink was because of drunk texting, that wasn't the truth. Well I guess it's partially true, but not the full truth."

I tell her about Damian, the drunk driver, and my vow for sobriety. I'm not really sure what exactly made me feel I could trust her with this information, maybe it's because I'm sitting on her bed, or the fact that she told me about her family issues. Whatever the reason, it feels like the right thing. I feel like I could trust her with anything.

"I-I'm really sorry that happened to you," says Fiona. "That's really terrible."

"Yeah, I don't like to tell people about it. It makes me feel like I'm looking for their sympathy."

"Whenever I would go to my grandma's house, she would always have all these candles. Every time I'd go I'd see a new candle. When she passed away, I started collecting candles in her memory. So I understand where you're coming from," says Fiona while inspecting one of her candles.

Of course Fiona would understand my feelings. She understands me, she gets me. I'm glad I chose to tell her about Damian.

"So your friend Sam, does she interrogate every guy that you bring over like that?" I ask.

"No it's just, since the break up with my ex, she's been super protective of me. I was in a really dark place, her and some of my other friends really helped me out of it. You're the first guy who I've..." Fiona stops herself and an expression flashes on her face like she's almost revealed too much information. "I've been trying to avoid men since the breakup for the most part."

"Well I think you're great, your ex just sounds like an asshole," I say. "I couldn't imagine losing a girl like you." Damn I meant to keep that last part in my head. Whenever I'm around Fiona, and look into those golden brown eyes of hers, I feel as if I've been injected with some kind of truth serum that makes me spurt out whatever's on my mind.

"So you're saying you wouldn't have cheated on me like he did? Wow, you must be one in a million."

"If I was in his shoes, I would've stayed faithful and proposed like a week in," I say. "You know, I mean like if I had a girlfriend who was as cool as y–I mean if I had a girlfriend I liked as much as–I mean if I had a cool girlfriend who was like you but different." I stammer, feeling heat rising to my face. My God I'm such an idiot, can I not just have a normal conversation? No way she's not freaked out now.

Thankfully, Fiona just laughs at this outburst, appearing to be unfazed by my awkwardness. I'm sure she's just used to having this kind of effect on guys now. "Anyway, how do you think the presentation's gonna go tomorrow?" asks Fiona.

"Ugh, I just want it to be over. I have a habit of crumbling under pressure during presentations."

"I remember you saying that, I'm sure it's not as bad as you think it is though."

"If anything it's worse. I get all sweaty and shaky and stuff."

"Well, this time I'll be there with you. I'll make sure you do well," says Fiona confidently.

When I first met her, Fiona was like a fairy tale to me, too good to be true. I never could've guessed that underneath my fantasy of her, the real deeper version of her, was even better. I'm not sure how the presentation tomorrow's gonna go, but I definitely feel a lot better knowing Fiona will be there with me. Tristan likes to say I'm his good luck charm, well maybe Fiona's mine.

THE BRAVE AND THE BOLD

It's the day of our big presentation. I'm sitting in class trying to keep myself from shaking. The way I feel before a presentation reminds me of how I feel when it's cold outside and I didn't bring enough warm clothing. My muscles are so tightly wound that I feel like a spring. I feel on edge, my teeth are clenched together, and I'm so jittery that I feel as if my whole body's vibrating, similar to how it feels when you're shivering on a cold day. Somehow though, I'm also sweating, a cold sweat that so far has only affected my palms, but once I actually get up in front of the class, it's sure to take over my face in a very visible, very embarrassing, show of social awkwardness.

"You good?" Fiona asks, with a knowing expression on her face.

I respond with an unintentionally curt nod, and then go back to staring out into space, trying to imagine I was anywhere else.

My mind continues to go back and forth between the upcoming presentation that looms over me like a guillotine, and the situation with Camryn and Tristan. It's like I'm in a pinball machine of pain. I wish that we were at least one of the first groups to present today. That way I could have a quick, merciful death instead of this elongated torture.

I don't know how I'm going to do this. Even under ideal circumstances this presentation would be a tall task, but now my brain's all scattered, my nerves and anxiety are higher than ever. I know I have to find a way though. If not for me, then for Fiona. I know how badly she needs this presentation to go well, it's worth 45% of our final grade. Normally I would just try to speed read from my index cards, and try to pretend that no one else is there, but our professor has continuously emphasized how important it is for us to seem like we know the information we're presenting. If it seems like we're reading or reciting, we'll get points deducted.

"Okay, thank you. Group five, please come up," says the professor.

It's finally our turn. Forget butterflies, it feels like I have fire breathing dragons flying around inside my stomach, and they're angry. We make our way to the front of the class, and I feel dozens of pairs of eyes on me. Full of scrutiny and judgment. They feel like lasers burning into my skeleton from all angles. When we get up in front of everybody, and face them, I get the full force of their stares. It feels like I'm shrinking with every passing second. My chest feels tight, my legs feel shaky, my face is burning and damp with sweat, but somehow the rest of my body is cold. The air in my lungs is becoming more and more constricted as if I'm fighting Darth Vader, and being choked by some invisible force. My heart races as if it's running the last leg in a 4 x 400m relay. I can feel the anxiety attack coming on, and I'm powerless to stop it. I feel like I need to go outside to get some air, but I obviously can't, it's the middle of our presentation. I feel like I might collapse at any moment. I'm so caught up in my head that I don't even hear Jack give me the signal that it's my turn to talk. Fiona, who's standing next to me, nudges me to get my attention. Here goes nothing.

It starts off about as well as you would expect. My voice is shaky and quiet. Even though I've spent countless hours going over what I'm supposed to say, I cling to my index cards like it's the side rail at an ice skating rink. This is awful, I feel like I'm dying. I can only imagine how disappointed Fiona is seeing this meltdown firsthand. I feel like curling into the fetal position and asking everyone nicely to stop looking at me. As I stand there, fantasizing about somehow acquiring invisibility powers, I feel a tap on my back. It's Fiona. In the millisecond that it takes for me to quickly look in her direction, she gives me a small reassuring smile, as if she could sense how uncomfortable I was. Considering my current performance, that isn't saying much. Still though, the small gesture means the world to me. It's as if I've been struck by a lightning bolt, but instead of being vaporized and dying instantly, I'm rejuvenated. It's the way I felt when we played cup pong that one time at the tailgate. Fiona's presence gives me strength.

The rest of my presentation goes by better than I could ever have expected. I'm still sweaty, but my words come out loud, clear, and confident. I don't feel like I'm about to become a Roman puddle on the ground, I'm able to stand tall knowing that Fiona's standing next to me. I feel like I'm John Cena cutting a promo. Completely in control, completely in my element. Before I know it, it's over, and since we were the last presentation of the day, we get dismissed soon after we get to our seats.

"Hey, thank you for helping me out back there," I say as Fiona and I walk out of the class.

"It's cool, I could tell you were struggling. You did great though."

"Yeah I had the class in the palm of my hand."

Fiona rolls her eyes. "Settle down there, you were good, but not that good. I didn't realize how bad your anxiety was though."

"Honestly if you hadn't been there I don't think I could have gotten through it," I say, trying to avoid her gaze. "But on another note, do you want to go somewhere to get food with me?

Somewhere off campus, to celebrate this monumental accomplishment?"

I hear the words coming out of my mouth, but I can't believe it's me that's saying them. It must be a residual effect from the presentation. I'm filled with an unbridled feeling of confidence.

"Sure, we can. You want to go right now? I'm free."

"Uhh I actually have my internship soon, it's my last day there for the semester. How about after that though? For dinner maybe."

I don't realize what I'm saying until it's too late. Based on Fiona's facial expression, she realizes it too. Her eyebrows shoot up as if it's Halloween and we're in a haunted mansion. A dinner between two people at an actual restaurant...that seems like a date. Surely she won't be comfortable in that kind of setting with me.

"Yeah, sure that sounds cool. So around 7?"

"Uhh yeah, that works," I say, hardly believing the events that are transpiring. "I can pick you up."

Before leaving my internship, Dr. Phillips gave me a $50 visa gift card to thank me for the work I'd done over the semester. It'll definitely help me pay for this dinner date or dinner non-date that I'm going on with Fiona. Just the confidence boost I needed.

I made it back to my room after the internship. I'm combing through the clothes in my closet looking for something to wear. I wish I could call up Camryn for advice on what to wear, where I should take Fiona, and whether or not this is even a date. Sadly, I still don't feel comfortable talking to her or Tristan. They'd just throw me off my game, and things are actually going well for me today. I don't need anything throwing me off. I end up picking out a tight fitting navy blue sweater, with olive green chino pants. Fancy enough for a date, but casual enough for some deniability.

Fiona and I made it to the restaurant. I decided to take her to Noir, which is a steak restaurant that's kind of fancy, but not too fancy. Fiona's wearing a black turtleneck with light blue mom jeans. A basic outfit, but she somehow looks more radiant than ever. Her beauty is magnetic. There's this aura around her that seems to draw attention effortlessly, especially mine.

The waitress leads us into the restaurant, to a table that's stationed right in the middle of the dining area. Right underneath a chandelier that feels like a spotlight. I can feel my skin itch with discomfort, but I have to tough it out. I don't want to wimp out in front of Fiona again.

"Is it possible for us to move to that table over there?" Fiona asks, gesturing to a booth in the corner.

"Yes ma'am. I can have someone clean that off for you. Just wait here a moment," says the waitress before briskly walking off.

"What was wrong with the other table?" I ask as we get escorted to the corner booth.

"I just like booths more," says Fiona, giving me the same knowing look that she gave me earlier in the day before our presentation.

It's almost spooky how easily Fiona was able to read my mind and see that I didn't want to sit at the first table that the waitress selected for us. I don't think I've ever met anyone that understood me so completely with just their intuition as a guide. I don't think even Camryn and Tristan would know that I'd want to move to a different table if they were in the same situation.

"This restaurant is pretty nice," says Fiona while looking at the menu.

I try to mask my concern when looking over the prices on the menu. I can tell this dinner is going to take a large chunk out of my wallet even with the gift card, but there's almost nothing I wouldn't have given to be able to go out to dinner with Fiona. So it's worth it.

"Yeah, it's a special occasion. The end of the semester, the end of that tiring project."

"Ugh, that project sucked. Jack and Aaron were dragging so much, I hate having to carry people."

"I guess I can't complain too much, it gave me a chance to meet you."

"Oh, whatever," says Fiona, flashing me with that brilliant smile of hers. The one that anyone would kill to have, the one that looks like it's worth even more than a million dollars.

"How are things with your comic going? I've been meaning to ask."

"They're good, I submitted my comic into the competition, so I just have to wait to see how I do."

Practicing my drawing with Fiona has helped significantly. I can tell she's seriously talented, and I haven't even seen any of her actual artwork yet.

"I'm glad I could help. You're still coming to my art show right? I'm excited to show you some of my stuff."

"Yeah, I'll be there. Just got to pick out my tuxedo," I say with a slight grin.

Fiona rolls her eyes. "Okay, James Bond."

Sitting at the table with Fiona feels as natural to me as breathing. Any trace of awkwardness or nervousness escapes me when I look into her eyes. The closest thing I could compare it to was when I was hanging out with Camryn, but with Fiona there's this...tension. As if we're opposite charges that are drawn to each other.

Our food gets to the table. I ordered salmon, and Fiona ordered pasta primavera.

"It's funny how we're at a steak restaurant and neither of us got steak," I say as I take a bite of my salmon.

"That's what you get for bringing a vegetarian."

"Next time we can go to a breakfast spot, I love breakfast food."

"Next time?" asks Fiona with a raised eyebrow.

I don't know what's gotten into me today. I keep saying things without fully thinking it through. This level of boldness is not my forte. First asking Fiona to dinner, and then asking her to a second semi-formal meal? This newfound confidence is nice, but I think I might be getting ahead of myself.

"I—I mean, if you want. If you don't, that's cool too. It can just be like a friendly thing. Nothing too serious," I say, stammering while looking down at my plate.

"You can be weird sometimes. You know that?" says Fiona, laughing.

"What can I say, you bring the weirdness out of me."

"Yeah yeah yeah, I'm sure you're plenty weird without me too," says Fiona.

"Well yeah, I mean I'm making my own graphic novel. I'd say that's pretty weird," I say with a shrug.

"Nah, that's not weird at all. I respect anyone that goes after their dreams like you are," says Fiona, pausing to take a sip of her water. "Your comic is really good too. Like if I didn't know you and I read your comic, I would think you were really talented."

After she says this I feel this shift in my head. I've been so private and protective over my work for so long. Too self critical to imagine anyone else actually thinking it was good, and not just saying it's good to make me feel better. I didn't realize how important her opinion was to me in this regard. Hearing her praise validates everything. It's worth more than any competition award could ever be. Even if no one else likes it, the fact that she likes it, is what matters to me.

"Thank you for that. I'm sure I'll be blown away by your art show. I can tell you're an incredible artist."

Really anytime I get to see Fiona it's an art show, because she's so beautiful that she's a work of art by herself. I decided to keep that thought to myself though, saying that out loud is a level of boldness that I haven't reached yet.

Fiona and I are sitting outside her apartment complex after dinner. Usually at the end of a date, or non date, or whatever this dinner was, I like to end it as soon as possible so I don't mess anything up, but right now I don't want Fiona to leave.

"You can pull into a park if you want," says Fiona as if reading my mind for the hundredth time today.

After finally fitting my car into a parking space (it took me 3 tries), I turned to Fiona. "Okay, so the other day you said that Tristan's not your type. What is your type?"

"You really held on to that, huh," says Fiona.

"It's not everyday I meet a girl who's not obsessed with Tristan."

"Okay, fair enough," says Fiona with a chuckle. "I like guys who are softhearted, and kind of quiet. Someone who's interesting and not afraid to be themselves. Pretty much the opposite of my ex. He was more the playboy type, which is how I feel Tristan is too."

Her description sounds kind of like me, but I'm too afraid to ask for confirmation. I can only imagine how embarrassing it would be to ask her if she was talking about me, and then for her to say no. There's something satisfying about hearing a girl I like say that she's not interested in Tristan though.

"Is that what your brother is like? I remember you saying he was an introvert."

At that moment it started to rain. I can hear the steady rhythm of raindrops hitting the ceiling of the car. It's a hypnotic sound, a calming sound. It makes Fiona seem even more pensive and thoughtful as she considers the question being asked.

"Yeah I guess you could say that. He's the best person I know, but he's quiet. My parents always try to push him into things he isn't ready for, and I guess I feel responsible for speaking up for him as his older sister. You kind of remind me of him in some ways."

I briefly consider all the times she's looked out for me in the past couple of weeks. Helping me with my art, helping me get through the presentation, helping me beat Tristan. It makes sense that it would be because she sees some of her younger brother in me. It's instinctual for her. That's the only explanation, I can't imagine that there's any romantic reasoning involved. Still though, if she thinks her brother's the best person she knows, and I remind her of him, that must be a good sign of something.

"Well he's lucky to have a sister like you. I'm lucky to have met someone like you too."

"Thank you," says Fiona. It's hard to tell because of the darkness that surrounds us, but it almost looks like she's blushing. "Do you have any siblings?"

"I'm an only child, but Tristan's been like a brother to me. We've been friends forever—well up until recently I guess."

"Oh no. What happened with you two?"

I turn away to look out the rain drenched window. "It's kind of complicated, I don't know, maybe it's just me being too sensitive."

I know I've felt as if I've been filled to the brim with valor all day. The boldness I've shown has been more than I thought was possible, but I don't feel daring enough to bring up what happened with Tristan and Camryn. How can I possibly explain that I had feelings for this other girl who then chose Tristan over me? Maybe it's because deep down I still feel inferior to Tristan, I don't know. What I do know is that here's a girl who likes me on some level, maybe more than she likes Tristan. I don't want her to view me as lesser than once I tell her what happened.

"Does it have something to do with that red-haired girl?"

I laugh. Her question snaps me back into focus. "No no, things with me and her are over."

If I was unsure before, today solidified it. Even if Fiona only ever likes me as a friend, which seems likely, there's no way I could go back to Olivia when I know there's a girl that makes me feel as good as Fiona out there.

"Well I'm sure whatever it is, you guys can work it out," says Fiona with what almost sounds like a relieved tone in her voice.

When Fiona finally went into her dorm, I looked at the clock on my phone and realized that we'd been talking in the car for almost three hours. It felt like twenty minutes. I considered confessing to her my feelings right there in the car, it was kind of the perfect time. We just went to dinner together and had a super intimate conversation in the car afterwards, but I got too caught up in the moment, and chickened out. Luckily for me, there's an even better time and place to do it. Like her art show. I can just picture it now, I go in looking all suave, with flowers and a hand-written letter detailing how I feel about her in vivid detail. Very romantic. On the flipside there's a chance I get publicly humiliated, but honestly, if she's not worth the risk, no one is.

THE MELTDOWN

It's a few days after the presentation, and the dinner with Fiona. It's the day of the big art show. I have a bouquet of flowers. An assortment of yellow roses, and sunflowers which are her favorite type of flower. I decided against bringing chocolates and the love letter, because it seemed to be overkill, even for me. I've been reciting what I'm going to say in my head, but I know that once I see her, I'll forget everything.

I know I joked the other day about wearing a tuxedo, but I seriously don't know what to wear to an art show. I don't think that jeans and a t-shirt's going to cut it, especially not if I'm going to be declaring my love for Fiona. I picked out a blue dress shirt and a checkered tie, with gray slacks. Luckily for me, I decided to invest in some nicer clothes after I got my internship. I didn't want to walk into the office wearing the same white shirt every day.

The phone rings, it's my dad calling.

"Hey, Rome. When are you coming home for winter break?"

Because of the divorce, I usually end up spending most of the thanksgiving break with my mom, and the weekend with my dad.

For winter break it's usually the opposite. I spend most of winter break, and Christmas with my dad, and then I spend the last few days of the break with my mom.

"I was planning on leaving Saturday night. I've finished my exams, but there's just some important things I have to tie up."

"Important things? You're done with your exams, and your internship doesn't start back up until next semester, so what important things do you have to take care of?" my dad asks with an air of impatience in his voice.

My dad is usually a patient and considerate man, but as an only child, one of the side effects of the divorce is that I often feel like my parents are in a constant tug of war, and I'm the rope they're pulling on. If I'm supposed to be with them for a certain amount of time, neither of them likes it if it gets cut short for any reason, including me arriving late because of a very important art show.

"It's just this art show. A friend of mine invited me, and I promised I'd go."

"A friend of yours? I know it's not Tristan, that boy doesn't have an artistic bone in his body. Is it that Kailey girl you were hanging out with over the summer?"

"Her name is Camryn, and no it's not her."

"An art show huh. Well you must really like this person to want to stay on campus longer than you need to."

"Yeah uh I don't know, she's cool I guess."

I'm crazy about Fiona, but similar to how it is with my mom, I feel kind of awkward talking about girls with my dad. It's not like I can tell my dad about her. It's always so embarrassing when I tell my parents about someone who ends up not liking me back. They'll be asking me about her for years after she rejected me. No, I'll pass on that.

"Well I'll let you go now. I'll see you in a couple of days," says my dad. "Oh, wait, before I go, is Tristan around? I want to say what's up."

We almost got through the full conversation without bringing up Tristan. Luckily he's out at practice right now. The team has a big holiday tournament coming up, and he's been out of the dorm more often than normal. Although now that I'm thinking about it, that could just be because he's hanging out with Camryn. It probably is that actually.

"He's out right now, but I'll let him know you called," I say.

My voice sounds insincere even to me, but I hope my dad doesn't catch it. I'm definitely not ready to talk about Tristan with my dad right now.

"Ahh, well okay. Good luck at your art thing," says my dad before hanging up.

Once I get off the phone with my dad, I start getting ready to go. I could really use one of Camryn or Tristan's pep talks right about now, but I'll just have to give myself one. I feel really on edge and nervous. Normally in situations like this I'd be feeling like I just want to get it over with. Especially when it comes to approaching a girl in a public setting like this one. That's how I felt the first time I tried talking to Fiona. It felt like too good an opportunity to pass up, but I didn't really want to do it, I just wanted to be able to tell myself that I gave it my best shot. Now though, it's different. I'm not dreading talking to Fiona tonight. It's more like the moments before getting something you've wanted for a long time. Like how it feels as a kid the night before Christmas.

Fiona is the walking embodiment of beauty and grace, and she's way out of my league, but part of me feels confident about how things will go tonight. It's like I try to tell myself that I have no chance with her to lessen the blow if things don't work out in my favor, but a significant part of my brain genuinely thinks I have a shot. The usual sliver of hope that I feel when it comes to women, is more than just a sliver this time. Maybe it's because we've spent so much time together over the past few weeks. Whatever it is, I have a good feeling about tonight.

A large part of my life I've been passive, and even though I've been trying to take a more active role in my life, specifically my love life, I've still had a lot of lucky breaks. The situation with Jade was pure luck, I didn't make it happen for myself, things kind of just fell into place. Same thing with Olivia, I mean she practically asked me out herself, I didn't even have to ask for her number. Tonight is my chance to actually take things into my own hands.

I make my way to Laguire, which is the building where the art show is taking place. It's the building where most of the art related classes take place. I've actually never been inside it before, but there's a first time for everything. It's a chilly night, the crisp December air nips at my exposed face. I'm grateful for this because it means I won't be all sweaty when I get to Fiona. At least not at first, I'm sure the sweat will start to fall at some point during my big declaration of love. I'm carrying the bouquet of flowers I got for her. For something so light, it's been pretty cumbersome carrying them around campus, but I'm sure the look on her face will be worth it when I give it to her.

As I walk into the building, my nerves build up even more than I thought was possible. For one, I definitely overdressed, a shirt and tie was not at all necessary for this event. I see plenty of people with just a long sleeve shirt and jeans. I stick out like a sore thumb, but I push forward deeper into the building. Fiona wanted me to be here, I'm determined to be there for her, and to finally tell her how I feel.

I round a corner, and there she is. Fiona, as radiant as ever. There's a small group of people around her, admiring what must be her work, but she's facing towards a tall figure. He's wearing a durag, sunglasses, and baggy sweats. It's Dalton. Fiona talks to him for another minute or two before Dalton takes out his phone and hands it to her. She then types something in. Dalton takes back his phone, and walks away with a smug grin on his face.

"Oh, hey Roman, what's good? Shorty just gave me her number," he says, gesturing at Fiona before walking off.

I stand there frozen, like an idiot, holding the flowers that I brought for Fiona. My mind flashes to that day a few months ago when Olivia walked out of Dalton's room, while wearing his shirt. No way the universe is cruel enough to put me through that again right? But it just happened, I saw it with my own eyes.

In that same moment Fiona turns her head, and sees me for the first time. Her jaw drops, a look of surprise crossing her face, and what looks almost like shame. Her eyes bulge as if trying to communicate something with me telepathically, but I'm not in the right state of mind to understand what it is.

Before she can take a step towards me, I race back out of the building, dropping the flowers I brought into the trash on my way. My mind is cloudy, I don't feel in full control of my body, but I know I want to get as far away as possible, and fast. I somehow made it back to my dorm, but I don't know how. I stumble into the elevator, and collapse on the floor, momentarily forgetting to press the button to my floor.

Once I make it to my room, the full force of what just happened hits me all at once. My eyes burn as I try to blink away the tears that start to cascade down my face. I feel this stabbing pain in my chest, my heart aches. I can't believe what just happened.

As I'm sitting there in my room, a montage of the events of the last few months plays in my head. Jade ghosting me, Olivia having sex with Dalton, Tristan and Camryn, and now this. Everytime I think things are different, everytime I think things are working in my favor, I'm shown that they're not. These girls that I thought cared about me, obviously don't. And how could they? I'm pathetic, a loser. All of these different people have been showing me that that's the case, it must be true. There's always someone they like more than me, I'm nothing but a joke. There must be something wrong with me.

I've broken many bones in my life, but this feeling is much worse than any of those injuries. The pain I felt after seeing Olivia with Dalton, and after seeing Jade on a date with that guy back over the summer is nothing compared to this. I realize now that it's because I cared so much more for Fiona than Jade or Olivia. The fact that someone as angelic as Fiona could choose someone as grotesque as Dalton says volumes for how she must view me.

Now I'm sitting here alone, with no friends to turn to, no work to distract me. I feel like I'm trapped at the bottom of a well, with nothing except this unbearable pain to keep me company. And that's when I hear it calling me. What do people usually do when they're faced with an unbearable emotional burden? They drink. Tristan's alcohol is calling to me like a proud parent at a sporting event. I stumble my way to the kitchen where Tristan keeps his alcohol, and grab a bottle of Captain Morgan.

I've been sober for my whole life. I've never had any alcohol, I've never smoked, I don't even drink caffeinated drinks. Partially because I feel as if I have an addictive personality, partially because I'm afraid of what I'd do if I got drunk. Who knows what this demented brain is capable of once my cognitive system is impaired. More importantly though, it's a way of honoring the memory of my cousin Damian. I couldn't save him that night, but a part of me feels like not drinking is a way for me to carry on his memory. That doesn't matter to me now though, I just don't want to feel this pain anymore. I don't think I want to feel anything anymore. I need to find a way out of this inescapable yearning that I feel. I've never felt more broken.

I go to turn my phone off so I can avoid sending any drunk texts, when I see I got a text from Fiona. I have my phone set so that I can't read the message unless I actually open the message, so I just see Fiona's name with a heart emoji next to her name on my phone screen, which is how her contact has been saved for the past few weeks. What could she possibly have to say? "Sorry Roman, you were cool, but compared to Dalton's raw masculine magnetism, you just come up short." Yeah that sounds like a nightmare. I ignore her message and delete her number, and then turn off my phone. There's nothing left for me to say. At this point I hope to never see her again.

The first sip goes down like acid. The burning sensation temporarily distracts me from the emotional pain I had been experiencing for the past hour. Other than the stinging in my throat, I feel pretty much the same, but at the same time I feel completely different. Sort of like how it feels when you drive through a new time zone, or walk around a new country for the first time.

I can no longer tell people that I've never had alcohol before. Throughout my college life, I've been to tons of different parties where people were heavily drinking, and I was just standing there in the middle of everything, completely sober. Observing everything around me. This always made me feel like I was cool, different, special even. I used to tell myself that my tragic backstory made me kind of like a superhero, and my vow to not drink gave me superpowers or something. Well now I'm not special, I guess I never was really. I'm just an ordinary person, actually maybe I'm even less than ordinary. An ordinary person wouldn't spend so much of their time trying to convince themselves that they're more than what they are. Maybe that's the message the universe has been trying to send this whole time. I feel like a pig rolling around in the muck, stuck in filth and unable to get out. Maybe this is where I belong.

These thoughts are running through my head as I take my next sip, and the one after that, and the one after that. Soon I feel my feelings start to dull, I wouldn't say I'm happy exactly, but the pain I felt earlier isn't as sharp. The spiced rum that packed a potent cinnamon punch, now seems to be losing flavor. The ensuing sips haven't burned my throat as much either.

Half of the bottle is gone, and I'm feeling pretty good, this drinking thing isn't so bad. As a matter of fact, I think I'll call Fiona, and tell her how I'm feeling. Well, after I go to the bathroom that is, my bladder suddenly feels like it's about to explode. I attempt to stand from the couch, feeling satisfied with my work, when everything starts spinning. I feel like I've just entered into a fight with Dr. Strange. I stagger to the bathroom. The bathroom is only a few feet away from the couch I was just sitting on, but it's the most difficult walk of my life. I feel like I'm on an episode of *Wipeout*. I finally make it to the toilet, and the rest of the night is a blur.

THE MENDED FENCES

I wake up the next morning on the couch in the living room area, with the half empty bottle of Captain Morgan on the coffee table. I feel extremely sluggish, and my head is pounding. Other than the physical discomfort, I feel an overwhelming sense of guilt. I feel as if I betrayed my cousin somehow, like I disrespected his memory by drinking, and maybe I did. Just another reason to feel like a worthless piece of shit. It's a long list at this point.

I do a quick check to make sure I'm not missing any body parts or anything, and thankfully nothing seems to be amiss. As I look for my phone, I hear a key in the door, Tristan must be back.

"Roman...have you been drinking?" Tristan asks as he walks in and takes a look at me.

"Uhh, what would give you that impression?"

"The open, half empty bottle that's right in front of you. Also this voice message that you sent to Camryn," Tristan says holding up his phone.

I hear my voice, or at least an extremely slurred version of my voice, playing over his phone's speakers. It's a minute and a half of me telling Camryn about my feelings for her, and saying her and Tristan would be better off without me in their lives. The ending has me drunkenly declaring "fuck the basketball team," as if I'm a member of the NWA in the 80's.

"I asked her to send it to me, so that I could play it back for you," says Tristan.

"Well, you know, that could be anyone," I say.

I don't explicitly remember making the call, but it makes sense given my inebriated state from last night. I imagine I got my phone trying to call Fiona, but thankfully I deleted her number before I started drinking. Unfortunately this left Camryn to take the brunt of my wrath.

"I knew you were upset, but I didn't know it was this bad," says Tristan with a sympathetic expression on his face. "I know how much it meant to you to stay sober."

"Yeah, well, don't give yourself too much credit for my melt-down."

I fill Tristan in on what took place the night before with Dalton and Fiona, and how I decided to drink as a way of numbing the pain I had been feeling.

"Why didn't you call me? Or Camryn? Or someone? Before the drinking started I mean."

I sigh. "You know things have been awkward between the three of us recently."

This is pretty much the first time Tristan and I have spoken since that night at Harris Teeter when he told me what was going on between him and Camryn. I'm a naturally non confrontational person. I knew this conversation with Tristan was unavoidable, at least if I wanted to keep my friendship with him, but I have been dreading it.

"Only because you made it that way. You know there's no bad blood on my end."

"Tristan, do you know how hard it is to always be in your shadow? To always have people look at me as your sidekick? I get it, you're Tristan, you're Mr. Popular, you're the people's champion. There's nothing wrong with that, in fact I even respect it. You haven't let that get to your head and make you any less of a friend. But it's still hard for me. I finally found someone who viewed me separately from you. Someone who didn't view me as a sidekick, and now that's gone forever."

There's a moment of silence as we both digest what I just said. Even I didn't realize how much pent up resentment I had accumulated over the years. There's no stopping me now.

"For the record I've never thought of you as my sidekick," says Tristan. "And Camryn doesn't either."

"That's cool, but you guys aren't the only people that exist in the world," I say. "And I appreciate that you felt guilty about it. You thought that I had feelings for Camryn, and you were right, but the fact that you thought that I had feelings, and went through with it anyway doesn't make it better. If anything it makes it worse. You could have any girl you want, why did you have to pick this one?"

"I'm sorry, man. Things just happened. If it was up to me, I would've picked someone else, but things just happened so quickly," says Tristan, his voice full of remorse.

"It's okay. It's childish of me to make you guys' relationship all about me. I just needed some time away to process things I think. It's my own cross to bear. I can picture y'all being good together."

"Well you don't have to worry about our relationship anymore, we both thought it would be best if we ended things," says Tristan.

"Why would you do a dumb thing like that?"

"I don't know, we both thought it would be better for you if we weren't together anymore. We thought it would be the best way to salvage our friendship with you."

Of course Tristan would do something like that. I know how long he's been looking for someone like Camryn to show up in his life. All the women he went through to find one he thought was the right one for him. From my perspective it seems like a nice problem to have, but it hasn't been easy for him to find someone he likes as much as Camryn. And he was still willing to give all that up for my sake. Even when I want to be mad at him, it never lasts, Tristan has a good heart.

"Tristan, that's ridiculous. The damage has already been done. You guys ending things doesn't do anything except make things super awkward for all three of us instead of just me."

"Well I mean it's too late now. Not like I can just message Camryn saying I was joking or something."

"I'll talk to her okay? Y'all don't have to do this for me. Just give me time to work things out on my own. I think I might need AA or something."

Tristan laughs, as we both feel the tension that has been present for the past week or two, start to evaporate. "AA for what? You had one drunken night, I'm pretty sure they'd kick you out of AA if they heard that."

"Maybe it'll be good for me. I feel like shit right now, I doubt I'll ever drink again, but I still think I have some issues I need to work out," I say with a shrug.

"Okay, well you work with therapists right? Why don't you set up an appointment?"

Therapy could be good for me, but I'm afraid that the therapists at the office where I intern might be judgmental of me. I don't want them thinking about me having a meltdown while I take their coffee orders.

"We'll see about that," I say hesitantly. "Also good luck in your tournament."

"Yeah man, imma get buckets," says Tristan with a grin.

Later that day I decided to call Camryn. She already went home for break, and I've never been to her house, so calling's really my only option. I'm not really sure how she'll respond. In her mind I basically ended her relationship with Tristan, and I've ignored her texts over the past couple of weeks when she was trying to reconcile. She has a right to be upset, but I know this isn't something I can avoid. It's an elephant in the room that needs to be addressed similar to how it was with Tristan.

If there's one thing my breakdown from the night before taught me, it's that I need Tristan and Camryn in my life. People who I can turn to when I'm down, people who generally have my best interest at heart.

"Well look who it is," says Camryn over the phone. "I thought you didn't drink."

"I don't, or at least I didn't, I don't know it was just a rough night for me. I'm sorry about the voicemail I left last night. I'm sorry I've been avoiding you for the past couple of weeks too."

"I understand you were hurt, but you can't just freeze your friends out any time they do something that you don't like."

"I know, I feel bad, but I just felt betrayed. Imagine being compared to someone your whole life and always coming up short. I know you guys didn't mean for it to happen the way it did, it just caught me off guard. Being friends with Tristan my whole life has made me sensitive towards this kind of thing."

"Look, Roman, I didn't–I don't want you to think I chose Tristan over you, that's not how things worked."

"I know, I talked with Tristan about it. We worked things out. He told me y'all ended things."

"Yeah, we didn't want to destroy our friendship with you over it."

"Well I think it's dumb. I mean if y'all like each other, I think you should go for it. I know Tristan must like you a lot."

Camryn pauses. "You think so? I don't know, part of me feels like it's not worth the risk. I mean if things go on longer, and then don't work out, it'll mess things up for all three of us forever."

"I know you know Tristan can be a bit of a player, but he's secretly been looking for love for a while now. He's gone through a lot of people that weren't right for him before he got to you. I don't want him to feel he has to sacrifice his happiness for me."

I remember the defeated look on Tristan's face over the summer when he talked to me about how he thought he lost Liz. I can only imagine how much worse it would feel for him to lose someone like Camryn. There's no way I can live with the guilt of knowing I'm responsible for that.

"Are you sure you're cool with it?"

"I'm sure, I was being childish before, but it doesn't matter what I think. It's okay for you guys to take your own happiness into account," I say. " If it makes you feel better, the three of us can meet up or something over break after Tristan's tournament."

"Yeah, I'd like that. By the way, what made you drink last night? You were like the king of sobriety."

"It has to do with Fiona," I say with a sigh. "I went to her art show thing, and brought these flowers and I was going to tell her how I felt about her, but then I saw her give her number to Dalton, and so I left. I was feeling hurt, and alone, so I turned to the alcohol."

"Ugh, I'm sorry to hear that. I was really rooting for y'all. You're never alone though. You'll always have me or Tristan."

"Yeah, I liked her a lot. I know I say this a lot, but I really felt I had a shot with her by the end. I mean we went to this dinner a few days ago, and we were talking in the car afterwards for hours. It was nice."

"Where did you take her?" Camryn asks.

"Noir. I don't know if you've been yet, but it's this steak place."

"And you paid?"

"Yeah, I mean I invited her so it just seemed like the right thing to do."

"Roman, that sounds like a date."

"I don't know, I mean it was never clarified. Even if it was, it must not have gone well if she's out here giving out her number to other guys."

"Well did she say anything after the art show? Like did she explain herself at all?"

I think back to last night. Me standing there, with my stupid little flowers, with my stupid little tie, frozen in place watching as the girl of my dreams gives her number to someone else at an event that she invited me to. I remember the look on her face when she realized I was standing there. An expression that almost seemed like it was pleading for me to stay, like she was trying to reach out to me telepathically to tell me something. I don't know, I must be misremembering, she was probably just surprised to see me. Maybe the fact that I was dressed so formally, holding flowers threw her off.

"She texted me but I ignored the message and deleted her number."

"Uhh why did you do that?" asks Camryn. I can hear the scorn in her voice. Even though it's under bad circumstances, it feels good to have this kind of conversation with Camryn again. It feels like it's back in the summer and we're at the thrift shop, breaking down one of my dates with Jade again. Simpler times.

"I'm not sure what she had to say, but I can only picture it being something bad. It's not worth the risk."

"Roman, we just talked about you not freezing out your friends," says Camryn.

"This is different, though" I say, my voice dropping to almost a whisper as a fresh wave of pain washes over me.

"Maybe she's like Jade, and she's into dating multiple people. I know things with Jade didn't end well ultimately, but you had some good times right? I imagine you're glad you didn't let things end when you saw her out with that other guy."

"But this is different," I say again. "Jade didn't invite me to the movies with her and then give another guy her number while I was there. Plus I just...liked Fiona more than I liked Jade. Fiona is just like the coolest girl I've ever met, I think."

"First of all, ouch. I thought I was the coolest girl you've ever met. Secondly, if you feel so strongly about her, that's just more of a reason to see what she has to say."

"I don't know. I think this was a sign from the universe to pull back. I think I was flying too close to the sun, and this is my punishment. It's probably best if I just move on."

After getting off the phone with Camryn, I feel a lot better. My relationship with my two closest friends are stronger than ever, at a time where I need them the most. But I still feel this lingering pain around me, like I just suffered a great loss. I try to tell myself there will be other girls. I mean life goes on, it's silly to think that this is the last time I'll feel this way about a girl, but I have this nagging feeling that Fiona is special. That I'll never find another girl that I feel as strongly about. I've spent my whole life feeling misunderstood and overlooked, and I finally met a girl who understood me, a girl who made me feel seen, and of course she just happens to be the most beautiful girl I've ever seen. If I let that thought take over my mind, it will devastate me. I have to try to find a way to move on, but I don't know how.

THE LOOK THAT KILLED

It's February, close to Valentine's day. The new semester has been pretty uneventful, nothing close to the excitement I experienced in my social psych class last semester. I don't have any massive crushes on any of my current classmates. I haven't spoken to Fiona since I saw her and Dalton together. I've deleted her number, and unfollowed her on all social platforms, a clean break. It was hard at first, it still is. Even with the support of Tristan and Camryn, whenever I let my guard down, I still feel this aching pain in my heart. I've been going to therapy, which has helped some too.

"So what do you guys have planned for Valentine's day?" I ask.

Tristan, Camryn, and I are sitting around at the dining hall. It's rare for the three of us to get to hang out like this together, because Tristan usually has a basketball related activity. It's still a little weird being around them as a couple, they always give each other these lovey dovey looks. It's nauseating to me, but in an endearing friendly way, not the jealous way I felt when they first told me about their relationship. Over winter break, the three of us got together and talked things out. Things aren't exactly back to normal. It's different now that they're together, but not different in a bad way. In fact, our friendship as a group has gotten stronger because of what we went through. It's almost crazy how easily we were able to mend our issues. Looking back, it all seems kind of silly. It's their first valentine's day as a couple, and I'm looking forward to experiencing some romance vicariously through them.

"I have an away game earlier that day, so I don't know. We'll probably end up doing something on a different day," says Tristan.

"Come on guys, you know I've been low on romance recently. I need y'all to have a good Valentine's day. If not for you, then for me," I say.

"What about Vanessa? I thought you guys had a good thing going?" says Camryn casually as she dips a fry in ketchup.

Vanessa's a girl that Camryn met in the black student union organization that she joined early in fall semester. Camryn set up a blind date for us a little over a week ago. Vanessa is cool enough, and she's pretty cute. She seems to like me a lot, but I'm not as into her as I'd like to be. She's the safe pick, but she doesn't do it for me like Fiona did. She doesn't make me feel understood, or seen. I've gone on dates with a couple of other girls over winter break, and at the start of the new semester, but it's been the same issue with them too. There's just something missing, on paper they're good for me, but I find myself unsatisfied and almost bored with the whole process. It seems the hopeful spark that I once had is gone. With Jade and Olivia, things were new, and fresh. I wanted things to work with them, of course, but part of me was just happy to finally be in the game. Things changed when I started getting closer to Fiona. She became the new standard for what I look for in women, but so far no one has come close to reaching it. I'm finally starting to see what Tristan went through for so long. Meeting different girls but feeling unfulfilled with all of them, except for one. The one that you think you blew it with. With him it was Liz, with me it's Fiona. Tristan eventually found Camryn, but I'm still looking for that person that surpasses Fiona in my mind. I'm starting to think that person might not exist.

"She's cool, but I don't know, I'm just not super into her. I don't think I want to spend Valentine's day with her. My therapist says I should keep my options open and keep playing the field. I guess I'll just keep doing that."

"Well a friend of mine said that one of her other friends is having a little get together on Valentine's day, so maybe we can go to that," says Camryn with a shrug.

"I'd be cool with that, not like I'll be doing anything else."

"Oh, Roman, when do you hear back about that comic competition thing?" asks Tristan.

I've been on pins and needles for the past week, waiting to hear back about the comic I submitted. I don't really know what to expect, I feel like the comic I submitted is better and has a better chance than the first competition I entered into, but you never know how things will play out. It's like after you take your SAT for the first time, and then study and do all those practice tests so that you improve your score whenever you take it again. But if you end up getting the same score, or maybe even worse, it'll ultimately just feel pointless. Hopefully I end up doing better this time.

"I'm supposed to hear back any day now, I'm really nervous."

"When will you let us read it? I'm sure it's fire," says Tristan.

So far the only people who have seen my comic are Dante, Wayne, the people who are judging the contest, and of course, Fiona. I want to know that it's good before showing it to my closest friends who I'm sure will talk it up and make it seem like it's better than it is.

"If I get one of the cash prizes this time, I'll let you guys read it," I say with a sarcastic laugh. My comic may have gotten better, but going from seventeenth place, to the top five is a bit of a stretch.

"Well it looks like we're sitting here with the next Stan Lee," says Tristan with a grin.

"Yeah, I'm sure all the ladies will be so impressed by that," I say while rolling my eyes.

"Fiona was impressed wasn't she?" asks Camryn.

I put my head in my hands. "She was a special case. I don't think I'll find someone like that again."

"Roman, you know better than anyone that I was saying the same thing for a long time, and then I found Camryn," says Tristan. "Or really, I guess you found her. That just proves that you're the ultimate wingman. Like I've been saying all along."

"Well, maybe I need to be the ultimate wingman for myself," I say jokingly.

"You know Tristan and I will be here to help you any way we can," says Camryn.

"Yeah, Roman I know what it's like to be in your shoes, but if anyone can make it through this, it's you," says Tristan.

It's been a rough few months for my love life, but I feel lucky to have people as good as Tristan and Camryn on my side with me.

After lunch at the dining hall, I go back to my dorm. I'm supposed to have a class later, but the professor made it optional, so I'm skipping it. I open my laptop, and check my emails immediately. For the past few weeks, I've been obsessively checking my emails to see if I got an email back regarding the competition. I scroll through a few useless alerts, and spam emails, until I see it, an email from the Stan Lee Comic Contest. I feel my palms start to sweat from the anticipation. My eyes stare, unblinking, at the screen. Should I open it? I mean obviously I have to open it, but am I ready to right now?

Waiting to hear back has been hell, but it's also been kind of nice. Up until now I could fantasize and daydream about having a successful comic. In these fantasies, I win this competition, or at least place in the top five, and then eventually I get a publishing deal. Maybe Marvel or DC see the comic and become so impressed that they try to buy the licensing rights for the character. Now though, there's no more fantasizing. Either I did well or I didn't. Realistically I'm hoping to get into the top ten. I may not be able to use it to my advantage in my dating life, but it would mean a lot to me.

I'm not religious, and I don't believe in prayer, but if there's a higher power I hope they're looking out right now. I open the email, and see that I...finished in fourth place! I can hardly believe what I'm seeing. My jaw drops to the floor. Fourth out of three hundred participants. It doesn't say anything about any sort of licensing deals, but getting fourth place means I win $800.

I think back to all the comics I've read growing up. How many superhero shows, and anime I've watched. I never would be in this position without being exposed to those things. I feel like my whole life has been preparing me to be a comic book writer. There's a part of me that's sad though. After all, there's no way I would've done this well without the art training that Fiona gave me. I wish I could share this moment with her, but I know I can't. Tristan and Camryn will be happy to hear about it though. I guess I have to show my work to them now.

I make my way to the gym, still on a high from the email I just received. Whenever I feel my emotions get too high or too low, I either need to eat, or go to the gym to level myself out. In this case, the gym is probably the healthier option. I'm practically buzzing with energy as I make my way into the gym. I can tell this is going to be a good workout.

I go to fill up my water bottle before my workout. As I'm standing there, I notice a group of three girls making their way down the hallway past where I'm standing. There's a tall darker skin girl that looks somewhat like Normani on one side, a short light skin girl on the other side, and in the middle is the unmistakably gorgeous Fiona. Her dark, curly hair is tied into a ponytail. Even though she just got done working out, she still looks great.

It's my first time seeing her since her art show in December. Fiona's striking features temporarily stun me into paralysis. I quickly pretend to look down at my phone as her and her friends approach me. Similar to that day when our group had to present our project in front of the class, I found myself wishing I could turn invisible, wishing I could be anywhere else. I remember learning that if you encounter a bear in the woods, it's best if you stay really still and try to play dead. They say that in nature, the most beautiful things are often the most deadly. If that's true, then Fiona is way more dangerous than a wild bear. I don't have to worry about a bear using my heart as a punching bag. Although I guess a bear could maul me and eat me, but a shredded and partially digested face is nothing compared to a broken heart. I can't exactly play dead, but maybe if I stay really still and pretend like I'm busy doing something else, she won't notice me.

It doesn't work. Now she's close enough that I can smell her cinnamon and vanilla scented perfume. I can tell she sees me without looking up. I feel her gaze on me like Superman's heat vision. Should I talk to her? I don't even know what I would say, but it feels like I should say something. Maybe I should ask her how things are going with Dalton. No, that would be weird. Maybe she'll say something to me first, I mean communication is a two way street after all. Although I guess she did try to text me and call me, and I ignored her, so if anything it's my move. Ugh, this is too complicated, I think I'll just say hi. Yeah, that's easy enough, just one word, I can manage that.

I look up from my phone to see that Fiona and her friends are fully within earshot, even for someone with a somewhat quiet voice like myself. We make eye contact and I...I lose all of my nerve. I feel like an actor that forgot their lines. Before I know it, they're past me, and out the exit.

VALENTINE'S DAY

"Are you still going to the Valentine's day party tonight?" I ask Camryn over the phone.

It's Valentine's day, I've never had a Valentine before, and it's looking like another loveless day for me on the most romantic day of the year. I figure going to a kickback is better than spending the night alone, watching reruns of *Seinfeld* and trying not to think about Fiona.

Oh, Fiona. The scene from the other day at the gym has been playing in my head almost nonstop. Like two ships passing in the night. It's crazy how you can spend so much time with someone, and they can mean so much to you, and a couple months later you could be complete strangers. Except unlike strangers, there's a certain energy when you walk past someone you know. In a case like this one, there was a coldness. Something as chilling and bitter as the winter air. It really felt like she was expecting me to say something, and then once I didn't, it was like some declaration of war.

"Yeah, you want to come?"

"Yeah, I think so. Vannessa's not gonna be there right?"

Camryn laughs. "No, not that I know of. Was she really that bad?"

"She's cool, I mean she's a good person, but she just wasn't the one for me. Oh, also guess who I ran into at the gym the other day...Fiona."

"Oh, wow, really? How was that?"

"I didn't-uh I wasn't able to say anything to her, so it was pretty awkward. We both knew the other person was there but neither of us said anything."

There's an awkward pause. The call is over facetime, but neither of us is showing our faces, so I can't see what facial expression Camryn's making."Oh..." says Camryn.

"I don't know why, but it feels like I've done something wrong. Fiona's the one that hurt me, but she's the one who seems more upset."

"Well, you did ignore her back in December, and from her perspective, you ignored her again."

"Yeah, but what am I supposed to say? Am I supposed to apologize to her for breaking my heart?"

"I don't know, Roman, but I do know what it's like to feel ignored by you, and it sucks."

The thought that I could have somehow prevented all of this pain and anguish, would be too much for me to bear. I can't imagine that Fiona's actually been suffering as much as I have though.

"She was probably just embarrassed thinking about all the time she spent with me."

Camryn laughs again. "Come on now Roman, don't be ridiculous. You know that doesn't make any sense."

Camryn is right, I do sound kind of crazy saying things like that, but what other explanation is there? I may have thought we had a connection, but we obviously didn't. Why else would she give Dalton her number?

"Maybe things just weren't meant to be. Maybe the universe set that whole scene up the other day to show me that things are really over between us and I should just forget about her."

Camryn sighs. "Maybe. I still can't believe that she was into Dalton. At the tailgate she seemed so cool and chic. I wanted to be her friend."

"Yeah. It is what it is I guess. I think I'll just do my best to avoid her from now on."

Camryn and I walk up to the apartment. I can hear music playing faintly in the background. The difference between a kickback and a full blown party is the scale. Kickbacks are typically more laid back, with fewer people, which I like. Either way I tend to keep to myself, but I feel more comfortable in kickback settings. Maybe I'll even meet someone tonight, it is Valentine's day after all.

As we get closer, one of the apartment doors opens, and a short light skin girl walks out. She looks familiar, but I can't place where I know her from. As she walks by us, I notice that she does a double take, and types something on her phone. Weird.

The door opens, I look around to take in the surroundings. For some reason the front door opens into the kitchen, it seems like there's not a lot of people there yet, which is good. I hate walking into a room and feeling a bunch of different eyes on me. Camryn goes in, and I follow, but right before I step in is when I notice her.

Sitting on a stool by the counter, directly across from the door, is Fiona. Her honey brown eyes lock on to mine for what feels like an eternity. The sparkle that normally accompanies them is replaced by something with a darker, more ominous undertone. I'm frozen. I feel like a zebra that realizes it's attracted the gaze of a hungry lioness. Any sudden movement will surely result in my death, or at least an embarrassing moment that's just as bad as death.

It all clicks, the girl in the hallway is one of Fiona's friends, Sam. The one I saw at the tailgate, at Fiona's dorm, and at the gym the other day. She must've texted Fiona to warn her I was coming.

I feel Camryn tug on the sleeve of my sweater. "Roman, what's going on, come inside."

I don't know how long I've been standing here, but I realize now that my freeze up has attracted the attention of the whole apartment. Somehow Camryn doesn't seem to have noticed Fiona. I feel my cheeks burn from embarrassment, as I take a step inside the kitchen area. I can feel myself start to sweat, it feels like the kitchen is a million degrees. Maybe it's just because of Fiona, I can still feel her eyes on me, like a hawk.

Camryn goes off to mingle with some people she knows, and I'm stuck there in the kitchen trying to decide what to do next. Maybe her being here is a sign that I should talk to her. I mean she's here on Valentine's day instead of off on a date with Dalton, that's gotta mean something right? Ugh, no, Camryn's here too, because Dalton and Tristan are both at the basketball game.

Maybe I should just talk to her, it's been a couple of months now, and I still miss her. Maybe I should try to just be friends, or at least clear the air. But I just...can't seem to bring myself to go over there. My mind flashes back to that night in December. The night my heart broke for the first time, the night I went against my lifelong anti-alcohol vow. Do I really want to open myself up to that much hurt again? For someone that will probably never be able to match my feelings?

As I stand there in the kitchen, I still feel Fiona's penetrating gaze on me. I feel vulnerable, and exposed. As if I just wandered into the middle of a shootout with no protection. I can't go through the rest of the night like this. I go over to Camryn, to let her know I'm leaving.

"What's going on? Are you okay? We just got here," says Camryn with a concerned look on her face.

"Yeah it's just…yeah I'll tell you about it later, don't worry about me."

"Okay, well text me when you get back."

As I leave the apartment, I feel my head start to swim with all of the different emotions that I've tried to work through and ignore over the past couple of months. My heart begins to ache as if it's back to that night again. My therapist tells me to stop being self deprecating, but it's hard not to have at least a slightly negative self view when you know you blew it with a girl you really like. If I was better, if I was stronger, I would've talked to her tonight. I would've talked to her at the gym the other day. Hell, I would've been able to have a normal conversation with her last May when I first met her. Maybe if I wasn't so weak and pathetic, she wouldn't have felt the need to run into Dalton's arms.

I make it outside, and I'm grateful for the fresh night air. Thanks to global warming, it's not excruciatingly cold like it should be considering it's still technically the middle of the winter. The apartment complex is close enough to campus that Camryn and I were able to walk over instead of drive, which I'm thankful for, because now I don't have to wait around for her.

I consider going back to my room to change so I can hit the gym to help clear my head, but my brain is so scrambled right now, that realistically that wouldn't help me at all. I definitely can't just go back to my dorm though, these negative thoughts would eat me alive. I wander around aimlessly for a while, before finding myself near the fountain in the middle of the quad. The same area where I consoled Camryn when her and Justin first broke up. The same spot where I saw Fiona for the first time.

There's a part of me that just wants to throw away my phone as far as I can, and just cut off all communication with the outside world. I could take a vow of silence, and become a monk or something. Maybe then I'll find solace.

As I sit there, plotting out my future residence in some remote, wilderness dominated, obscure stretch of land, I notice a familiar scent. Cinnamon and vanilla, the perfume that Fiona always wears.

"Hey, Roman," says a voice that sounds sweeter than a songbird's.

"Hey, Fiona," I say, as I feel my heart start pounding in my chest. It's the first time we've spoken to each other in a little over two months. "How did you know I was here?"

"Camryn came up to me, she was worried about you and told me that you like to come here whenever you feel like brooding," says Fiona as she comes to sit next to me.

"Well, you found me."

I'm not sure if it's my introverted nature, my social awkwardness, or a combination of the two, but I hate confrontation. I'd rather escape to higher ground, and live to fight another day than to face whatever's coming at me head on. It's probably why I have so much trouble speaking in front of a group of people, it makes me feel as if I've taken off my camouflage in front of an apex predator. Avoiding people is what I do best. It's what I did when Olivia gave me the ultimatum a few months ago, it's what I did when I first found out about Tristan and Camryn, it's what I did with Fiona at her art show, at the gym, and even at the party tonight. The closest I've come to a real confrontation was that time at Dalton's apartment, but even then I retreated. Now though, there's nowhere for me to run to. I frantically try to comb my brain to find some way out of this situation, but I guess this is just unavoidable.

Fiona sighs. "Look, Roman, you knew how much that art show meant to me. I specifically asked you to be there, and you just...left."

"I saw you give Dalton your number," I say, while looking down at my feet.

"But Roman, you didn't even give me a chance to explain myself. You just left without a word and never responded to any of my texts or calls, and then you just acted like I wasn't even there at the gym the other day, and then you just show up here tonight."

"To be fair I didn't know you'd be at the kickback, I would've stayed away if I'd known."

"That's the whole point though, you've been acting so cold to me. I don't understand why, I mean I guess I understand, but you didn't even talk to me about it. I thought we were friends," says Fiona, pausing to wipe her eyes. "Or maybe more."

Did she say maybe more? I must be imagining things, or maybe when she says "more" she just means like best friends instead of regular friends. I should be upset at her for guilt tripping me like this, but I hate seeing her cry. Knowing I'm the cause makes it even worse.

"I know you and Dalton are probably happy together, and that's cool, but I can't just be friends with you. Watching you with some other guy would be like torture for me. That night after I saw you two together, I...I drank. For the first time. I was in a really dark place, and yeah it was pretty awful. I can't be friends with a girl I feel that strongly about."

There's a pause as Fiona takes in what I've said. Her cheeks are wet from her tears, her eyes are starting to get puffy, and she's sniffling like it's the first day of spring, and she still manages to look hauntingly beautiful in the moonlight. There's an angelic, elegant quality that she has. Even now during this uncomfortable emotional discussion, I feel myself being drawn to her.

"I'm really sorry, I didn't know," Fiona says, gazing into my eyes as if trying to see if I've changed in some way since then. "You should know that I gave DJ a fake number. He's been trying to flirt with me all semester, and I was trying to get him to leave the art show as soon as possible."

I feel a swirl of emotions. Rage at Dalton for bothering her and making her think she had to do all of that to get him to leave her alone. Anger at myself for icing her out. But most of all, relief. The way it feels when you get to sit down after hours of standing up, or when you finally step into a hot shower after a long day. Her and Dalton aren't together? That means this is my chance, my chance to finally tell her how I feel about her.

"I'm sorry too. I was a real dick to you. I shouldn't have just tried to cut you off like that. I just thought it would be better for the both of us. I was really looking forward to your art show, I brought flowers and stuff for you too."

Fiona manages a small smile that makes my insides melt like a popsicle on a hot day. "I know, I saw them in the trash. I took them out and put them in a vase in my room."

I smile back, even more self assured that this is the right time to tell her how I feel. For once I'm determined not to chicken out.

"Oh, before I forget, I won $800 in the competition thanks to you, I finished in fourth place," I say.

Fiona's eyes light up. "Really? I knew you could do it. I've been trying to tell you how great you are."

I take a deep breath and lock eyes with Fiona. Usually it's hard for me to make eye contact with people, especially when I'm telling someone how I feel, especially when that someone is Fiona. Now though, I feel confident, I feel strong. Similar to how I felt after that reassuring smile Fiona gave me during our presentation.

"Fiona, I remember the first time I saw you. Last May, right over there," I say gesturing to a walking path that's about ten feet away from us. "You were crying then, like you are now. Your eyes were all puffy and you had tear streaks on your face, and I've still never seen anyone more beautiful in my life. I think I've been in love with you since that day."

However Fiona reacts to this, I'll be proud of myself. I finally worked up the courage to tell her how I feel, and I can live with knowing I gave it everything I had. I feel like my whole life has been building to this moment. A year ago, I could never dream of doing something like this, but now I feel at peace with it. I guess I should thank Jade, Olivia, and the other girls from the past who've hurt me, because I wouldn't be here if it wasn't for the lessons I learned from them.

Fiona flashes me the biggest, most radiant smile I've ever seen, putting the sun to shame. "I've been waiting to hear you say that since last May."

After those words leave her mouth, all we can do is stare at each other, drinking each other in like we've been stranded in a desert for days and we've finally found water. The preciousness of the moment is so immense that neither of us even dares to blink for fear that this spell will be broken. After what feels like an eternity, I finally lean in to kiss her. My dad was right, it feels as natural as breathing, it feels so much different than all the other kisses I've had. Fireworks go off in my head like it's the Fourth of July. It's the best sensation I've ever experienced.

When we finally pull apart, we both look at each other with these silly grins on our faces. I know I'm supposed to be with Fiona. I've never been more sure of anything in my life. Roman the romance addict finally finds love on Valentine's day, how fitting. I think to myself

"So does this mean we're like boyfriend and girlfriend now?" I ask.

Fiona rolls her eyes. "Duh," she says as she pulls me in to kiss again.

EPILOGUE

It's April now, a couple of months after Valentine's day. Since we've become a couple, Fiona and I have been practically inseparable. I've never felt more joyful and fulfilled. For our one month anniversary, Fiona made a painting of us sitting by the fountain in the quad. Recreating the moment that brought us together. Fiona also finally let me see the paintings she had on display at the art show that I missed, she's really a supremely talented artist.

Being in an actual relationship has been interesting. I feel such satisfaction telling people that I have plans with my girlfriend. So far that's definitely the best part of the relationship...just kidding. Of course Fiona is all I ever could have wanted. I often find myself wondering how I had made it as far as I did without her in my life. I used to worry that I had been alone for too long, and that I was too independent and wouldn't be able to fit myself into a relationship with someone. I tend to create space for myself from people, even with Tristan and Camryn sometimes, but with Fiona it's different. I feel like I always want to be closer to her.

The four of us, Camryn, Tristan, Fiona, and I, are sitting around together in the dining hall. The basketball season is over now, so we'll be able to hang out with Tristan more often. At the end of the month, the four of us are supposed to be going to a Drake concert together. Our first official double date. Tristan and I used to talk all the time about what it would be like when we both had actual girlfriends that we could do things with together. Now that day is finally here.

Seeing Tristan and Camryn together, looking so happy and at ease with each other after seeing them be unhappy for so long is refreshing.

"Oh, my gosh, Fiona, where did you get those earrings?" asks Camryn.

"Roman got them for me," says Fiona who gives me a loving smile.

Camryn and Fiona have gotten along perfectly. It seems like Camryn has developed some sort of woman crush on Fiona. Back in February, they decided to go get their nails done together so they could get to know each other better. When they came back, Camryn couldn't stop gushing about how cool Fiona was. They've been the best of friends ever since. Camryn even tried becoming a vegetarian, but ultimately gave it up after a couple of weeks because she missed eating chicken wings.

"Camryn, you gotta chill with the flirting. I don't want you to steal my girl right in front of me," I say with a grin.

Camryn laughs. "Well as long as you know I could have her if I wanted."

"I'm not ready for him to know about us yet," says Fiona jokingly.

"Camryn, you gotta keep your love affair in check. We still owe these guys an L in cup pong," says Tristan. "No more ducking smoke from us, Roman, basketball season's over and I'm ready to get my revenge."

Things with Tristan and I have been slightly different. It was awkward at first, but since our talk that night in December there's been an openness between us that wasn't there before. The talk turned out to be one of those things that you didn't realize needed to happen until it happens and then things are better than you thought possible.

"Fiona and I are more in sync now than we were then, if any-thing we'll beat you worse this time," I say with a shrug.

"Yeah yeah we'll see about that," says Tristan with a grin.

I've always felt like I was a lone wolf, left to fight my demons by myself. Longing to feel the love and acceptance that seemed to come so easily to everyone else. It always felt to me like there was a key piece of my heart that was missing, empty, waiting to be filled. Sitting here with the three people that are closest to me, my heart's never felt more full.

ACKNOWLEDGMENTS

Thank you Monet Lescow, you were the first person to read this book from start to finish and your positive review came at a time when I really needed to hear it. We barely knew each other at the time, but you still took the time to read over my work. I'll always appreciate that.

Thank you Ashley Rankin, for being in my corner and supporting my writing. Without you I probably would've given up on this book early on in the process. I'll always be grateful for your valuable input and perspective. A thank you goes out to Mike Roundtree and Whitney Ptiman, who also took the time to read the chapters I sent them while giving valuable feedback.

DeAjai Dawkins you understood the vision from day one, and you helped reassure me that my vision worked within the context of this book.

Thank you Danielle Jackson Shields, for helping me through the editing process and making this story flow smoothly.

And finally, thank you to my family who patiently listened to me ramble about my dream of publishing this story for several months.

About The Author

C-Trey Jones lives in Charlotte, North Carolina where he likes to spend his free time writing for his blog, going to the gym, and binge watching tv shows. He graduated from UNC Charlotte with a major in psychology and a minor in public health.

You can learn more at ctreyjones.com and @ctreyjones.

www.ingramcontent.com/pod-product-compliance
Lightning Source LLC
Chambersburg PA
CBHW031522310726
48971CB00008B/2330